# FINDING SOLACE

*The Finding Series, Book Four*

## CJ Allison

© CJ Allison 2017
This book is a work of fiction. Any resemblance to names or events that take place are strictly made up by the author.
Warning: This book contains situations and languages intended for mature audiences over the age of 18 only.

Cover design by Author
Cover photo: Reggie Deanching, R+M Photography
Cover Model: Matthew Hosea
Editing: Erika McCabe

*This book would never have been even written if it weren't for the absolute beautiful picture I saw and just pulled me to it. So Reggie and Matthew, this book is dedicated to you. Without that picture that is now my cover, this would have been a totally different book. Thank you.*

# PROLOGUE
## *Present Day*

I hear the announcement: now boarding flight 1090 non-stop to Baltimore Maryland...

Christ. I feel my palms becoming sweaty. I fight the urge to just run out of the airport. Fuck the price of the ticket. It's been years since I've been back home. I love my family, I just don't like that God damn town.

My best friend, pseudo cousin, is getting married and practically begged me to come home. She even went as far as asking me to be in the wedding. I can't ever tell her no. I certainly can't now since she says she's counting on me to be an usher.

This is the girl I still dream about but never can have. We aren't related by blood, but we were raised as if we were. She couldn't get past the feeling that it was wrong, and that broke my heart. I left home the moment I graduated and never looked back. Now I have to watch her walk down the aisle into someone else's arms. Akia...

# CHAPTER ONE
*Reflection*

## ZEKE

Named Ezekiel James Boyd, I came out kicking and screaming and never really stopped. My parents, Samson and Jamie Boyd, learned about my pending arrival the day they told my sister her adoption was official. They had been trying for five years to get pregnant and pretty much gave up. My dad said it took five years, nine months, and two weeks for me to come into their lives. He knew I was going to be a hot head, determined to do things my way.

My mom didn't have any family that was close. Both her parents pretty much abandoned her. Her best friends were her family, and I grew up believing they were my aunts and uncles. I had several sets of grandparents, and I always felt loved. Mom always said, "The best family you can have are the ones you make for your own."

Mom's best friend growing up was Patience. Patience was married to Chance and they had a daughter named Akia. Akia was a year older than me and for as long as I can remember, I was in love with her.

We were the youngest of all the kids in this dysfunctional but amazing family. My nickname was Zeke, but Akia could never say it right. To her I was Zee. To me she was Kee, since I had a hard time pronouncing her name as well.

Zee and Kee, two young kids that were inseparable. I told her when we were five and six that I was going to marry her when we grew up. She would giggle and tell me I was silly.

"Cousins can't get married, Zee," she would say when we got older and understood the dynamics of our family.

"But we aren't cousins, Kee," I would argue.

I never gave up that dream of her being my wife one day. That dream was stomped on every time she had the chance.

When she started dating, I went insane. I can't tell you how many guys I would beat up to try to keep them away from her.

♦♦♦

From an early age, I had these feelings inside that I just couldn't explain. There was this uncontrollable need to get just get away from it all. My dad said that I had a fire in my eyes twenty counties wide. I later learned this was from a song that he used to sing to me. It was all true. I just couldn't see myself living in that small town. I wanted to go out and see it all.

When I graduated from high school, I saw my opportunity. My dad was a police officer, later promoted to detective. I was always intrigued by his work.

Computer Forensics was something that I thought was amazing. It was an opportunity for me to somewhat follow in my Dad's footsteps, yet set my own path. Although there were local colleges that offered degree programs, I looked into where the program was offered around the country and found one in San Antonio. That town was significant to my family because that was where a resort that all the parents would all go to every year as a tradition. The kids would all stay with one of the grandparents, rotating each time to try to make it fair.

When we were teenagers, the older kids explained what the resort was all about. It was a place that accepted all types of sexual orientations. It was a place where Uncle Bradley, Uncle Bruce, and Aunt Carrie could be completely comfortable. The family would go as support, and they all seemed to love the openness of the love that was felt there.

I learned later on that it was not "normal" to be married to both a man and a women. My Uncle Bradley, Uncle Bruce, and Aunt Carrie were just that and nothing more, my family. They had three kids, Michaela and William, who were twins, and then there's Charlie. As a kid, it didn't really seem weird, but as an adult, I look back and am still amazed at how they dealt with it all. No one knows who the dad is of any of the kids. To them they are both their dads.

You see, I never saw anything unusual. They are dysfunctional at best, but for me, they were my uncles and aunts. All I saw was a loving family.

Love was the predominate factor in the dynamics of our family. Love was what I felt every time I was in her presence. Real or not, I know I felt it for her. Akia, the girl who made me angry at her dismissal, the girl who I know felt something for me but refused to acknowledge it. We weren't blood, but she just couldn't get passed it.

One of the times the parents went on their vacation, I decided to put it all out there. I was sixteen and she was seventeen. I set up a picnic at the place my dad proposed to my mom. This little spot on the towpath has always been special. My dad comes here to reflect and it's a place we have shared family picnics.

"Zee, what is this all about?" Akia asks.

"Kee, sit down. Can we talk?" I ask.

"You know we can, but this is, I don't know, Zee."

"Listen, I need you to know. I have these feelings and maybe they aren't right, but we aren't blood. I...I think I love you."

I watch as she grabs her red hair, putting it into a ponytail, a sure sign that she's gearing up for a fight. Fuck. I try to back pedal and tell her that I'm kidding. The words that come out take me by surprise.

"Zee. You are everything. You have always been my best friend, my constant. You know I love you, but..."

Great, the "but" comes out. I push my hands into my pockets and find it hard to meet her eyes. I don't want to watch as she lets me down.

I feel her press herself against me and places her hand on my face, forcing me to meet her eyes.

"I have always loved you. We have a love that no one will ever understand. But...I can't. It's not right. I know we are not blood, but what will our parents' think?"

"Fuck them. I mean, come one! Like there's normal relationships in our family. We have a poly relationship in our mix for fuck's sake."

"True, but this can make our dad's angry. I know that they have taught us that love is love. However, I don't see them agreeing to this, I just can't."

I pull her closer and place my forehead against hers. She feels amazing in my arms.

Not knowing what really to do, I tentatively place my lips against hers. I can feel her shaking, but she doesn't resist. It's an innocent kiss at best but means the world to me that she let me in.

"Let's just enjoy this, okay. Face tomorrow as tomorrow."

"Okay, Zee, this really is amazing. I've never had someone else do anything like this for me, ever," she says.

"I hope you never do."

# CHAPTER TWO

*Lessons*

## ZEKE

That moment I had at the dock will go down as the most amazing moments of my whole life. At least to this point of my life. Even when I lost my virginity, it wasn't as special as that little moment in time. Kee and I continued to talk every day and hang out together, but it wasn't the same. She acted as if that moment never happened.

You may wonder how I could have lost my virginity to someone else if I was in love with Akia. First, you have to understand how the teenage male mind works. All it took was hearing the douchebag that she was dating at the time brag about certain freckles in areas he shouldn't know about. After his face accidently slammed into a locker, I made a date with one of the girls in my class. It didn't take long after that before I was well on my way to being a douchebag myself, adding imaginary ticks to my headboard.

I saw Akia graduate. I was there for her party and sat in the background, constantly wanting to know how she was really feeling. My dad says that he is an empath, meaning he feels people's feelings, I guess I didn't inherit that. I had no clue what she was feeling, and I all I felt was loss. She was accepted to a nearby college to study veterinary medicine, but it was still about an hour away. We stayed in constant contact, which didn't sit well with the people we were dating. I say that was the reason I had so many girlfriends my senior year. Honestly, it was just me searching for a replacement.

I worked every moment I had at Uncle Bruce's mom's farm. I was able to save up a lot of money. I had plans to drive across the country to school. I was going to take my time and enjoy my summer before entering into the college life.

Kee came home for my graduation, and I tried to convince her to come along with me for the summer. During my party, I pulled her away from everyone to talk to her.

"Zee, it sounds amazing, but I can't. You know I have a boyfriend, and I'm planning on going back early to get an earlier start on classes."

"Boyfriend," I mutter.

"Don't start, Zee. That's not fair," she says, placing her hands on her hips.

"No. What's not fair is the fact that in any other fucking universe, I'd be your fucking boyfriend," I say, raising my voice.

"Please keep your voice down. Someone is going to hear you," Kee says through gritted teeth.

"I don't care who hears me. I don't care who knows. You're the one with the issue," I respond, throwing my hands in the air.

"Exactly. So, stop being an ass and leave it be," she says, stomping her foot.

"Now I'm an ass because I have feelings for you? That's rich," I say, laughing.

"No, *Ezekiel*. You are being an ass because you can't understand that this will never work," Kee says, getting into my face.

"Why not? Tell me one reason outside of our parents where this wouldn't work!" I snap back, looking down into her eyes. Our faces are so close our noses are almost touching.

"Because I don't feel the same way as you do, Zee!" Kee screams as she steps back. I can see the tears starting to form in her eyes.

My heart is pounding in my chest. I know she doesn't mean it. *How can she do this to me?* I can feel myself losing control. I flex my fingers in and out of fists.

"You keep telling yourself that, sweetheart," I say in a softer but bitter tone. "I'm done. Thanks for ruining my party."

I left her standing there by herself in tears and headed back to the party. My parents wouldn't let any of us drink, since we were underage, but man did I need something. I headed straight to the kitchen, where I knew the drinks were for the adults in attendance, and practically chugged down half a bottle of whiskey. My throat burned, my chest felt like it was on fire, but slowly I could feel the pain slip away.

I have both hands on the counter with my head in my chest as I hear the booming voice of my dad.

"There you are. Why the hell is Akia crying, and why do you smell like you just drowned yourself in alcohol?" Dad asks.

"Why don't you ask her why she's crying, since she seems to be able to lie without any issue?" I blow out a breath of air. "I really don't want to talk about it, Dad."

"Well, I don't want you drowning your apparent sorrows in the adult's liquor. Talk to me, Ezekiel, I know something has been going on. I'm not stupid," Dad says, pressing his hand around the back of my neck.

"She's just…nothing…she's nothing anymore. I asked her to tag along with me this summer and she acts like I'm asking her to marry me," I huff.

"And what are your intentions, Zeke? I know you care about her. I'm sure she knows, too. Does she feel the same way?" Dad asks.

"What do you mean? We are best friends. Of course, we care about each other. Dad, please. I really don't want to talk about this. I just want to hit something. I was going to wait a few days before leaving, but I can't wait. I don't want to be here anymore," I shrug.

"You know that's not going to go over very well with your mother. She's having a hard enough time as it is. Whatever is going on with Akia needs to be put aside. Don't hurt your mom. You know I won't be very easy on you if you do," Dad says as he slips his arm around my neck.

I think he's going to put me in a headlock, but he just side arm hugs me. "Do I need to go get your sister Destiny to calm your shit down, or are we good?" Dad asks.

"I'm not, but I will be. Even though right now I feel like I'm going to puke," I groan.

"Good. First lesson of adulthood. Don't guzzle down alcohol to try to drown your sorrows. I'm here for you, son. You know you can talk to me about anything. Now go apologize to Akia," he says.

"I didn't hurt her Dad, she hurt me. If anyone should apologize, it's her," I say, grabbing for a cup to fill up with water.

"Second lesson of adulthood and one I thought I had instilled in you over the years: the man always apologizes. If you make her cry, you apologize. Even if you don't feel like it's your fault, it is. Just fucking apologize. Believe me, you'll thank me one day for that little life lesson," Dad chuckles.

I look up and see Akia standing like she's lost in the backyard. As if she senses me, I see her glance up and meet my eyes. I can see the sadness there and it breaks my heart all over again.

"Can you see yourself never talking to her again? Never seeing her smile? Knowing the last time you saw her, you made her cry?" Dad asks, giving my shoulder a squeeze.

"No...when you put it that way," I huff. "But right now, I'm going to be sick." I duck under his arm and run to the bathroom.

I feel so stupid. Why the hell did I think it was a good idea to drink that whiskey? I empty the contents of my stomach and more before I feel like I'm finished.

I hear Uncle Bradley yell from behind the closed door. "Serves ya right, you damn punk. Drinking my whiskey without asking. Fucking lightweight. You'll never survive college at this rate."

"You are so mean. Leave him alone, and Aunt Carrie is looking for you," I hear Akia say.

"You're lucky, Z-man. If my beautiful wife wasn't in need of my presence, I was going to make you do a shot with me," Uncle Bradley yells through the door.

Just the thought of that makes me groan, which must have been loud since I hear Uncle Bradley laughing as he walks away. "I'll take that as a grateful groan."

I feel a cool washcloth being placed against my neck. I look over to see Akia sitting on the side of tub.

"I'm sorry," we both say at the same time.

"No, I'm sorry, Zee. I'm sorry that I can't give you what you want. I do love you, just not in that way. You always tried to get your way, you know? Do you remember when you were adamant that we would be married one day? I always thought it was just silly kids' stuff. You meant it though, didn't you? That time at the dock, you really were serious weren't you?"

"Of course, I was serious. I thought you understood that, that kiss, was real and I've never forgotten it. Have you ever known me to joke around about how I felt?" She shakes her head and goes to say sorry again, but I stop her. "Stop saying you are sorry, dammit."

"I can't lose your friendship, Zee. Please."

"Boy, today is full of life lessons, I guess." I huff.

"What do you mean?" Akia asks.

"Don't try to drown your sorrows in alcohol, you will only get sick. Say I'm sorry, even if I don't think it's my fault, and don't turn you back on your best friend, even if she doesn't love you. I'll always be there for you, Kee. No matter what."

I suck in my pride and gather myself together. Taking some ibuprofen and antacids, I make it through the rest of the night and end up having a really good time.

Watching my dad shake his head at my mom's antics with Uncle Bradley, I forgot about being sad. I looked around at the people in my life and felt a tinge of homesickness before I was even gone.

# CHAPTER THREE
## *Road Tripping*

### ZEKE

I waited a week before I finally decided to hit the road on my journey across the country. My pickup packed to the gills, I hug my parents goodbye and promise to check in every chance I can. I watch in my rearview mirror as my dad tucks my mom under his arm, pulling her in tight. I can see my mom visibly shake as she cries, tucking her face into his chest.

I feel a lump form in my throat as they slowly disappear from my view. Taking a deep breath and blowing it out, I look forward. I look over at my dad's guitar sitting on the passenger seat and smile. This is what I've been waiting for my whole life. I've mapped all the stops that I have planned. Three months of getting to see the country and experience something else outside that small town.

A little over seven hours on the road, I hit my first stop, Pigeon Forge, Tennessee. I spent a few days there taking in all the tourist sites that I could. From Dollywood, to the Hatfield and McCoy's Dinner Feud, I experienced it all. It was pretty amazing.

I checked in to places through Facebook and took a ton of selfies. Uncle Bradley would comment on each and every post with something totally inappropriate. My mom wasn't much better. Sometimes it felt like they had highjacked my posts, but it always made me laugh.

The next stop was Nashville. I spent almost a month there. I almost didn't want to leave. Even though I was only eighteen, the amount of alcohol consumed was astronomical. If it weren't for the posts, selfies, and check-ins, I would have forgotten most of my time there. The girls, wow. They sure as hell make them very pretty and very friendly. Daisy dukes and cowboy boots will never be the same in my eyes. I learned to line dance, and I met some up and coming country music stars. I even helped a band whose guitar player had come down sick by filling in for a few nights. The one thing I did get from my dad was his talent in playing the guitar and singing.

From there I headed to Memphis and then onto Shreveport. Last was Dallas before I was in San Antonio. I still had two weeks before my classes started, so the plan was to get a job and get moved in and settled into my apartment I rented off campus.

I received a call from Uncle Bradley who told me he had an interview lined up for me at the resort. Texting me the details, I immediately made a call to the General Manager of the resort and scheduled a day and time for the interview.

My apartment was within walking distance, so I decide to take in the sights and sounds of the city. Rounding the corner, I see the most magnificent sight. There is a large fountain that would rival any of those in Las Vegas, not that I've ever seen one in person.

Asking for Ms. Cartwright at the front desk, I'm asked to take a seat in the lobby. I can understand why my family loves this place. Uncle Bradley, Uncle Bruce, and Aunt Carrie must feel so open and free here. I look in awe at the openness of the guests. The smiles and laughter are welcoming. Before I have a chance to take a seat, I see the most striking older woman approach. She is in a tailored pantsuit with her platinum hair plaited down the center of her back. She is slightly taller than me in her heels, and I find myself trying to stand up straighter.

Her handshake is strong and I feel her long fingers wrap around my hand. I glance up and notice the rather large Adam's apple. I find myself staring at her impeccable skin.

"Ezekiel, I presume? You have Samson's strong jaw and Jamie's nose, a fine mixture. There are some good genes in your family. Please take a seat," Ms. Cartwright says.

"Please call me Zeke. I know this probably isn't appropriate, but you have such amazing skin." I'm embarrassed that I can't take my eyes of her.

"Lots of laser treatments. I haven't gone through the full change, but I'm on my way. You do know, right?" she asks.

Clearing my throat, I respond, "Yes, that's why I'm staring, you are stunning. I'm sorry. That's really rude of me."

"Not at all. This is the place to be open and honest. I wish people outside these walls would just ask sometimes. Plus, what women wouldn't want to be called stunning from a young buck like yourself? Anyway, please tell me you have your father's talent of singing and playing guitar. I see you breaking hearts like glass while you are here."

Hearing that phrase makes me smile. "My dad used to tell me that all the time. One of his favorite songs he always sang for me has that line in it."

"I know. It's still one of my favorites. I can remember him sitting with his guitar playing that right here in this lobby. He drew in quite the crowd. It brought tears to my eyes. He always played with such power and passion."

"To answer your question, I don't know if I'm as good as him, but yes, I do sing and play," I answer.

"Perfect. I'll have to hear you myself so I'm sure you don't hurt my guests eardrums, but I'm in need of someone to play a few nights a week. If that's okay with you?"

"I'm willing to work wherever you put me. Honestly, I'm a college student and what funds I did come with will be depleted soon. Plus, I took three months getting here. Let's just say, I enjoyed the trip."

"Well, since you are only eighteen, we will have to keep you mostly in the lobby, but we may be able to get you in the lounge a few times. As long as it's during dining times." She pulls a walkie off her hip and calls for someone named Dan to meet her in the lobby.

A younger man shows up with a folder. "Hey, I'm Dan. I manage the scheduling of the entertainment staff. Welcome aboard."

The rest of the day, I'm filling out employment paperwork, treated to lunch, and asked to come back the next day to play a little so that Dan and Ms. Cartwright, who insisted on me calling her Rachel, could ensure I was as good as I claimed.

The next day I played the song that my dad always sung to me, the same song he sang in this very lobby. I drew a crowd, received a thunderous applause, and a huge thumbs up from Rachel.

# CHAPTER FOUR

*College Life*

## ZEKE

I loved college. It wasn't really like school at all. I had a few academic classes that I would dread, but my major classes were the ones that made it exciting. I couldn't get enough. To be able to dive into a program, a hard drive, or operating system, and find the smallest of clues was gratifying.

Even though I wanted to make my own way, my family always seemed to be there to provide me opportunities. I continued to work at the resort and got to spend time with the family when they would come down on vacation. Dad and I sang a few songs together each time they were here.

My junior year, Dad found a way to meddle and get me an internship at the SAPD, San Antonio Police Department. I didn't get to assist in any real life cases my first year. I mainly worked in IT, fixing people's computers and resetting passwords. I wasn't going to complain though. The workforce was amazing. Especially Emma. She almost had the ability to make me forget about Akia. Almost.

Emma was first year cadet but had a six sense in reading people. She reminded me a lot of my dad. That wasn't a good thing. She always knew I wasn't completely hers. I tried. I really did. I did all the things you are supposed to do for your girlfriend. The first time Akia facetimed me when Emma was there, she called me out. Emma said she knew right then by the way my facial expressions changed.

"You love her. I can see it," Emma said.

"Of course, I love her. She's my best friend, family," I responded.

"No. It's more than that. You are in love with her. Zeke, it's okay. I always knew I was competing with something. I just didn't realize it was a *someone*. Does she know?"

I hung my head and nodded. "She doesn't feel the same. I know I need to move on. I just can't seem to do it."

"You are an amazing man. I'm so sorry you are going through this, but I'm not going to compete. If you haven't moved on with me, then you never will, and I'm not the one for you. I hope you find her one day."

Even though we broke up that day, we remained friends. I decided to date, but not get serious with anyone after that. I couldn't put another woman through what I had Emma. I never want to see that look of pity and pain from anyone ever again.

I graduated Summa Cum Laude with almost my whole family in attendance at the ceremony. Mom cried and Dad beamed with pride.

I searched through the group meeting each of their eyes and smiling. There was one set of eyes I was hoping to see, but they were not there. I could feel the smile falling off my face until I looked at my sister Destiny. The contrast between her caramel skin and light green eyes always had a calming effect on me. I regained the smile and a new sense of determination. I couldn't keep pining over the girl that I would never have. From that moment on, it was about me and my life.

# CHAPTER FIVE

*Present Day*

## ZEKE

I dig my boarding pass out of the front pocket of my backpack and sling it over my shoulder. Sending a quick group text to Mom and Dad, I let them know the plane is on time and I'm about to board.

They insisted on picking me up at the airport, even though I wanted to get a rental car. I'm going to be staying for two weeks and really don't want to rely on others to get around. Dad said I could use his truck, but I can't see him driving Mom's car. It's a Volkswagen Bug. I chuckle to myself thinking of him squeezing his body into that little hunk of metal. Better him than me, I suppose.

Scratching my chin, I think about what they are going to think when they see my full beard and shaved head. Apparently, I inherited Mom's genes since my hair started thinning out this past year. My dad and his dad still have a full head of hair.

I didn't want to be one of those guys who hold onto what little hair they may have, and just decided to shave it off. At least I never have to worry about hat hair. I have a baseball hat collection that can be considered an obsession.

Finding my seat, I tuck my backpack under it and lean back. Popping in my earbuds, I pull the bill of my hat over my eyes and let the guitar riffs take over my thoughts.

I fall asleep and miss the inflight snack. As if four small pretzels and three sips of soda would have been satisfying. I feel a hand on my shoulder and pop out an earbud. The flight attendant hands me a bag of said pretzels with a wink and asks me to prepare for landing.

I work the kink out of my neck and look out the plane's windows. I can see the mountain ranges to my left. I almost forgot how different the terrain is here versus Texas.

I'm in no hurry and am the last one to get off the plane. I follow the crowd to baggage claims with my head tucked and my music blasting in my ears.

I catch movement out of the corner of my eye and look to see my mom coming at me at full speed. You would never guess she was in her sixties. With only a few lines around her mouth and eyes, there's not a spec of gray in her shoulder length blonde hair. My dad however, has that salt and pepper hair.

I drop my backpack and take Mom into my arms, lifting her off her feet.

"Oh my God, Zeke. Look at that beard. Sam, you need to grow one of these…but I can't see your dimples," she exclaims.

"I can still get the ladies though, Ma," I laugh.

"Boy, you look good. Give your old man a hug."

I set my mom back on her feet and am engulfed in my father's arms. He may be old, but he is still strong as an ox. You don't realize how much you miss your parents until you are hugged by them again.

♦♦♦

We pull into the lane to my Gram Pam's, Bruce's mom who is everyone's mom or grandmother. I see the farm that I used to work at and smile seeing nothing has changed. It's like I'm seeing it through a new set of eyes. Everything is open and green and actually quite breathtaking.

I see a line of cars on both sides of the driveway. I guess the gang's all here. My family has grown since I've been gone. Most of all the kids are married with children of their own. Akia and I are the only ones left and that will soon be changing.

"Get in, they are all up at the gazebo," my dad says, getting into a four seater ATV.

No time to wind down, *great*.

We reach the top of the hill and I see kids of all ages running around. Then I see the wisp of red hair standing in the arms of a decent looking man. I say decent because…. well you know why.

I wait for the pained feeling to hit my gut, but it never does. It's the strangest feeling. My chest doesn't hurt. I feel...nothing.

"The Prodigal Son has returned!" Uncle Bradley yells, pulling me into a bear hug.

Chuckling I say, "First, I would have had to squander all of my inheritance, which I haven't. Second, I would have be coming home to stay, which I'm not."

"Z-man, you ruin everything. I like the scruff. Makes you look all rugged like a cowboy. If you were wearing a Stetson instead of that ball cap, you'd be a Texan stereo type."

The hugs seem to be endless. I'm anticipating hugging Akia, just to see if those feelings return. When it's finally her turn, I brace for the onslaught of emotions. Still nothing. It's a great hug. A very nice warm hug. But that's it. Just a hug.

I'm introduced to her fiancé Doug, who gives me a firm handshake and a welcoming smile. I don't even feel like punching him.

"Ezekiel. Get your ass over here and give us hugs. We're too old to get up for your ass," I hear someone yell.

Looking over, I see Sun and Flower, my Aunt Patience's parents, still dress up like hippies. I jog over and kneel down in front of them so I can hug them at the same time. Sun's hair is completely white but pulled back in his signature ponytail. There's a large bald spot sitting in the center of his head. Flower's hair is also still long and white, braided down her back. They still look good for being in their late eighties, although a little frail.

"I hear they grow some good stuff down there. Did you smuggle us any home?" Sun asks.

"It's not illegal anymore, Pops, but no. I didn't bring any home, sorry."

"Bah, what good are ya if you can't bring your grandparents home any good weed?"

I take an open chair next to Flower and sit down.

"Don't listen to that old coot. We still love you. Plus, he has plenty of his own," she says, patting my hand and laughing.

I look around at my family and finally feel something. Not what I was expecting to feel when I saw Akia again, this is different. I feel like I've missed out on so much. I've missed weddings and births and holidays. I've missed home.

# CHAPTER SIX

*Sky Blue Eyes*

I'm staying at the apartment above the garage at the farm. Mom wanted me to stay in my old room at home, but Dad thought I'd want to have my privacy. I'm thinking it's his privacy he wants. I cringe thinking that my parents are still having sex.

The morning sun blasts through the window making me groan. Hitting my phone to look at the time, I see it's early. The fact that it's two hours earlier than that on my body clock has me covering my head with a pillow. Unfortunately, I have to use the bathroom. So, I guess I'm getting up.

The kitchen is fully stocked and I'm grateful to see individual coffee pods next to the brewer on the counter. After making a cup, I walk over to the patio. There's a little table and chairs there, so I go out and take in the fresh morning air. Summer is winding down, so there's a little bit of fog rolling across the mountains.

I prop my feet up on the railing and look down to the barn. Movement catches my eye and I'm figuring it's the workers tending to the horses. I'm going to have to take one out to see if the farm really hasn't changed.

A soft feminine voice floats up from below and I find myself raising to my feet. I lean over the railing to try to get closer to the sound.

A woman exits the barn walking beside a horse carrying a bucket. I can hear her talking calmly to the mare but can't make out what she is saying. I take her in from head to toe. Work boots on her feet, snug fitting blue jeans that are worn in various places, a loose t-shirt with the farm logo on the back and a ball cap with a pony tail pulled through the hole in the back.

"Good morning," I say, lifting my coffee mug in the air.

I hear a high pitched squeak, see the bucket go flying in the air, and watch as the horse takes off towards the field.

"Holy shit! Who the fuck are you and why did you have to scare the ever living shit out of me?" she yells, leaning over and holding her chest.

I can't control my laughter. Until she looks up and I almost swallow my tongue. The most beautiful face is looking up at me with the most striking sky blue eyes.

"Well? Are you going to just stand up there and stare at me? Do you like scaring women and horses first thing in the morning?"

I finally find my voice and say, "Sorry, ma'am, just wanted to say good morning."

"Good Lord, you must be Zeke. Your father is the only other man who has ever called me ma'am. You look like him, too. Except you're bald and have a beard. Oh, shut up, Gracie, you are rambling."

"I'm assuming you are talking to yourself, so you would be Gracie, correct?" I ask as I run my hand over my head feeling the morning stubble.

"Grace, Gracie, Gracie Lynn depending on who is talking to me, yes."

"Squeak," I say smiling.

"Excuse me?" Grace responds.

"I think I'll call you Squeak."

## GRACIE

I love mornings. It's so peaceful on the farm. I'm holding an empty bucket that I need to drop off by the pen. Leading Lilly, my favorite mare, out to be walked, I'm hit with a booming voice. It seems to bounce off the barn and hit me right in the back of my head.

The bucket goes flying and Lilly takes off while I spew obscenities. Holding my chest and looking up to where I think the voice came from, I met with the softest set of brown eyes. He's unbelievably gorgeous. Standing on the balcony of the apartment above the garage, he's leaning over the railing, resting on his forearms that are covered with tattoos. He has a full beard and what looks like a normally smooth head. I can see the morning light bounce off some stubble.

This must be Zeke. Holy baby Jesus, why didn't anyone tell me he looked like that now? He looks nothing like the kid that was a year behind me in high school.

I had gone to my dad's last night and missed his homecoming party. I'm not family and felt uncomfortable in going anyway.

There's no recognition on his face. He has no clue who I am. I don't look the same either. I grew up and filled out. Little Miss Grace Lynn Myers. The gangly girl with braces and mousy dishwater blonde hair who hid behind glasses.

So, his choice of a nickname does not bode well. It reminds me of the teasing I had to endure as a teenager, not a term of endearment.

"Not a fan of my choice of nicknames?" he asks. "Looks like you bit into something nasty."

"If you only knew," my only response is a muttered one.

"I'm sorry, I didn't catch that. You need to speak up there, Squeak," Zeke says as he stands.

My mouth goes dry. Not only are his arms full sleeves, his chest is covered as well. He's wearing nothing but sleeping pants that sit low on his hips. I wish the railing and bannisters weren't in the way. I just know he has that infamous v. He places his hands onto the railing and I about choke when I see his pecks and biceps ripple.

"Cat got your tongue?" Zeke says with a smirk.

"Will you go put a shirt on? God, I swear if you spread your arms out, fucking wings would sprout out behind you." I slap my hand over my mouth realizing I said that out loud.

I hear him let out a low chuckle. Christ, even his laugh is sexy.

"More like the demon of orgasms," his face has a devilish smirk.

"What?" I gasp.

"What," he responds. "Why don't you come up and have a cup of coffee with me?"

"Um, I'm working. Plus, I need to go corral Lilly in that you sent running to the fields. Maybe I'll catch you later, Demon Zeke." I give him my best sexy smile. I probably look constipated.

## ZEKE

Holy shit. Thank God I had the railing there to hide my growing erection. I could literally feel her eyes traveling over my body with appreciation. I felt the hairs on my arms raise the same time blood seemed to shoot to my groin. I've never had anyone look that captivated. There was lust, but it felt different. Her eyes darkened and it felt like we were the only two people on earth.

When she called me Demon Zeke, it was like a pulse of electricity flowed through my body hitting every nerve ending. Instinctively, I reach down and squeeze myself to stop from coming in my pants. A pure carnal need is the only way to describe it.

I watch as she quickly turns, her ponytail swishing back and forth and am drawn to the sway of her hips and healthy sweet ass. Her arm goes up and I hear her say, "Morning, Gram."

Like a bucket of ice water, I glance over and see Gram Pam standing on her back porch.

"Goodness, Zeke. Do your parents know you have all that ink? Never mind. I have sausage gravy done and the biscuits are about ready to come out of the oven. Get over here and eat breakfast with me. I've missed you," she says as she heads back into the house.

Living in the south, I've tasted my share of awesome sausage gravy and biscuits. None have ever compared to Gram's. I just hope she hasn't lost her touch over the years.

I head in and snag a shirt, not bothering with shoes, and jog over to the house. As I enter the back door, the incredible smell has me stopping in my track. I take in a deep breath and smile.

"Let me help you Gram," I say.

"Oh hush, I may be old, but this keeps me going. Happy you are home, Ezekiel. Sit down and get ready to dig in. I think I still got it. Tastes the same to me at least, but hell, these old taste buds may not be the same." I watch as she gingerly bends over and grabs out the tray of biscuits from the oven.

I want to jump up and help her, but I know she would smack me in the back of my head if I did. I have a feeling it would sting just as much as it did when I was a kid.

"So, I see you met my Gracie. Sweet girl. Dedicated to this farm and the horses, but doesn't seem to have much of a life outside of that. You went to school with her, you know? She's a close friend of Akia's. She has a business degree and has been helping out William with running this farm. She refuses to stay in the office and insists on doing everything she can, wherever it's needed. She loves those horses. She's staying in Bruce's old room. Insisted on staying in the house and not the apartment. She claims it's because she doesn't want to be alone, but I know she thinks she's taking care of me. I don't complain, though. This house is big and I love having her around." I watch as Gram seems to go off inside her head in thought.

"Hmmm, I don't remember her. I wasn't close to many of Akia's friends, though. I couldn't seem to get past seeing just her back then," I say as I feel Gram reach out and pat my hand.

"And they call it puppy love…" she sings out. "Probably too old of a song for you to know, but that is what it was. We all saw it. The look in your eyes. The way you tried to protect Akia. You know, she felt like it was her fault that you left. She would spend time with me and we would talk. I know everything that happened between you two."

"It wasn't just her. Maybe a part of it, but Gram, I just needed to get away. I wanted my own life," I say.

"Oh, Ezekiel. We all knew you would venture out on your own. I tried to tell her that, but she always felt guilty. You need to know that. Do you still feel the same way?"

"I thought I did. Until I got here and saw her, hugged her, it was different. I think I'm finally ready to let her go." I shrug.

"Well, make sure you tell her that. It would be the closure you both need. She's so in love with Doug. Yet, I feel like she's holding back a little because of you. But enough of the serious talk. Eat up and tell me if ol' Gram still has her thing," she says laughing.

That first bite brings me back to the time I was here almost ten years ago.

"Amazing," I groan and watch as she smiles bright.

# CHAPTER SEVEN

*Closure*

## ZEKE

I really want to talk to Gracie after the conversation I had with Gram. I'm thankful to hear that she is taking care of more than just the horses around here. However, I think it's more urgent to speak with Akia now then to wait.

I came home early for the wedding, so I'm hoping she's not too busy to have a good talk. The phone call I make goes straight to voicemail, so I send off a quick text asking if Akia can squeeze me into her busy schedule.

I get a text immediately back that she is on the phone with the caterer and will call me when she's done.

I jog back up to the apartment and grab a quick shower, shaving my head back to smooth and wait for her return my call. I decide to throw on a pair of cargo shorts and a plain dark t-shirt. I slip on a pair of casual loafers just as my phone begins to ring.

"Sorry about that, Zee, final wedding prep is literally going to send me to the crazy farm. What's up?" Akia asks.

"Was wondering if you could squeeze your best friend in for a little catch up. I'd like to talk to you. I didn't have much time last night with everyone else around," I reply.

"I'm starving. Can we meet at the diner? It's near the floral shop that I need to stop by and wrap up a few things."

"That works. I just ate some sausage gravy and biscuits a little while ago, but I can watch you eat," I laugh.

"Oh my God, I'm jealous...and even hungrier now. I should be there in about five minutes. I'll meet you there." I hear the beeping of the car as she starts the engine.

"On my way, see you in a few," I respond, hanging up.

I'm understandably nervous and run through what I need to say through my head the entire drive over. Entering the diner, I see the red hair before anything else. Akia has already ordered and is stuffing her face.

Again, I wait for the gut punch. The feelings just don't come. It's really odd to say the least. I slip into the booth across from Akia and laugh as she puts up a finger while she chews and swallows.

"Sorry, I was starving. I didn't think you'd mind that I didn't wait. I ordered you an unsweet tea and a coffee. I wasn't sure what you preferred these days." She appears a bit nervous.

"Thanks, I'm going to go back to Texas twenty pounds heavier with Gram's cooking, I could do without the sugar," I say.

Instead of jumping right in, I decide to start off with talk about the wedding. "So, you ready for the big day Saturday?"

"I don't know if I'll ever be ready, but what's not done will work out. I'm excited to finally be Mrs. Williams," she smiles. "The guys are picking up their tuxes Wednesday and are going to hang out. Did Doug talk to you about it?"

"Yep, all set. This will give me some time to interact with him more. Facebook doesn't really give me a whole lot of insight. You look happy though and so does he. That's all that matters, right?"

"I am happy. He's really incredible, Zee," she says, not meeting my eyes.

"Listen, that's all I've ever wanted, Kee. For you to be the happiest girl in the world. I thought it would be me..." she tries to interrupt, but I grab her hands and give them a little shake, making her finally meet my eyes. "Let me finish, please. I love you. I always have, but something is different." I watch as she cocks her head in question.

"I waited for those feeling to hit me like a Mack truck when I saw you in person last night. It didn't happen, nor did it happen when we hugged. I never thought I'd get over you. Distance, life, maybe growing up, seems to have changed things. I also want you to know that you were not the reason I left. It's really not your fault at all. I know I said it was and blamed you, but it was really just me needing to find myself. I've always felt smothered here, you know that. I don't want to speak for you or think that I know what you are feeling, but I want you to know that I would never hold you back. You deserve your happily ever after. I will still always be your best friend. I will also kick Doug's ass if he ever hurts you, bet your ass on that,"

Akia squeezes my hands and blows out a breath of air. "Thank you. I needed to hear that. I really did. You know I love you, too, and am honored to call you my best friend."

"So, tell me about Gracie. I understand she is a friend of yours?" I ask.

"Damn, you move on quickly," she chuckles. "Gracie, huh? When did you meet her?"

"This morning. Scared the shit out of her coming out of the barn. It was quite the sight. Gram says she was your friend in high school, but I don't remember her."

"Her nickname was Mouse, although she didn't like it all that much. It was more of an insult in her eyes. She's grown up and changed a lot from back then. She never really gained her confidence, though. It's a shame she can't see how beautiful she is. I think she still sees that little mouse of a girl in high school,"

"Shit," I say rubbing my hands over my head.

"What?"

"Now I know why she looked at me like she had bit into something rancid this morning. Fuck," I mutter.

"What did you do?" Kee asks with a look of concern.

"Not what I did, what I said. When I scared her, she sort of let out this noise and I gave her a nickname because of it."

"Oh no," Kee says putting her hand over her mouth. I'm not sure if in shock or to hide her laughter.

"Oh yeah, I called her Squeak."

I see Kee's shoulders start to shake as she removes her hand and laughs. "Not a good start, Zee. I don't mean to laugh, but damn. You sure know how to impress them ladies, don't you? But you didn't know or remember. You can always go with that."

"Fuck. I feel like such an idiot. It was meant to be cute, but shit," I say, shaking my head. "I probably really hurt her feelings."

"It may have stung, but Gracie is strong and has a huge heart. I'm sure a simple apology will go a long way," Akia says, patting my hand. "At least I hope for your sake it does."

"What's that's supposed to mean?" I ask.

"Oh, you'll see," she says and nothing more.

✦✦✦

I take my time driving back to the farm. I decide to take all the back roads I used to drive when I was a teenager. It's almost like I'm seeing it through a whole new set of eyes.

Our town is nestled in the valley between two mountain ranges. There are curves and dips in the road that make you feel like you could go airborne if you drive fast enough. With the windows rolled down, I find myself cringing at the old feelings of those days. I can remember driving faster than I should have because I was angry. I wanted so bad to get away, I don't remember really enjoying the surroundings. The true beauty that this area has is really breath taking. I feel like I had blinders on growing up.

It's still early afternoon when I finally make it back. I decide to change into a pair of jeans and boots and head out to the barn. I'm hoping to run into Gracie but instead am greeted by one of the ranch hands. He's grooming a horse, preparing it to be ridden.

"Hey there, taking this one out by any chance?" I say in hopes I can take it.

"Sure am. You must be Zeke. Pam has been talking my ear off all week about you coming home. Interested in taking this old boy out? I have to warn you, though. He's a bit hard headed and likes to go full speed at times."

"That sounds just about what I need right now," I laugh.

I help put on all the tack and saddle. Once mounted, I can feel the muscles of the horse flex. This is one powerful beast, and it sends a rush of excitement through me. I used to love the freeness of being able to come here and ride whenever I wanted.

It's an American Quarter horse with a name of Zeus, which is fitting. I watch his ears closely and let myself get a feel of him as I direct him past the fenced in area to the open field.

Bending down to rub his neck, I whisper, "You ready to let loose, boy?"

I get a returned snort and watch his nostrils flare. Yeah, he's ready. I don't have to give much of a kick for him to take off at full speed. I let out a whoop as he picks up even more speed, the air rushing by me. We reach the top of a ridge, and I slow him down to a trot. I can see Uncle Bruce, Uncle Bradley, and Aunt Carrie's house in one direction and three other houses spread out in the other. Houses that were built after I left by their kids.

Slowing Zeus down to a slower pace, I take it all in. Each of the homes are nestled in their own little nook, giving them all a sort of privacy. Except for up here, you can see everything including the farm behind me.

It makes me wonder what it would be like to be able to just jump on a four wheeler to borrow a cup of sugar. To be able to just visit your family and enjoy their company whenever you feel the need.

A sense of regret overtakes me as I think I robbed my parents of this. I missed out on so much because of my selfish need to leave. Pulling out my phone, I dial my Mom and ask if I can come for dinner tonight. Of course, I'm met with a response that I'm always welcome and she looks forward to it.

I have a feeling that my visit is going to be for more than just a wedding. It's more like a chance for me to apologize for my actions. Actions I didn't think were that big of a deal, but now realize they probably had more of an effect than I would have thought or wanted.

I hand off Zeus to the same ranch hand as before and head up to grab the truck keys.

My parents built the home I grew up in before I was born. There was a little cottage that belonged to Sun and Flower, which had been passed down to all the aunts and uncles. My parents were the last to live in it. They started building as soon as they learned I was coming along. They never sold it though hoping that the next round of kids would be living in it as well one day. That's where Akia is currently living with Doug.

The one thing that I learned from my Dad was to always show up with flowers. My mom loved wild flowers, so I make sure to stop and pick her up a bouquet.

Entering the house, it looks the same as I remember. The furniture has been upgraded, along with the television that takes up most of the back wall, but other than that it's home. It still smells the same, too.

It's an open floor plan, so I can see my mom working in the kitchen. The smile she gives me lights up her entire face. I feel that twinge of regret again but shake it off and smile back.

There is nothing quite like a mom hug, especially when it's your mom who's giving it. I'm wrapped up in the familiar smell of perfume and again feel that sense of home.

I'm sitting at the counter making idle talk like I used to do when I was younger. Dad walks in carrying an almost identical bouquet of flowers that I brought.

I watch as he immediately goes to my mom and wraps her in his arms from behind. He whispers something in her ear, making her giggle. It's like déjà vu. This is the exact way he has always come home and greeted my mom. I can almost guess what he whispered. I smile and cringe at the same time.

"I see that face, boy. Like I used to tell you when you were younger, deal with it," Dad says.

"I'm dealing. It's sweet that you two still have it, just kind of gross being that you are so old," I respond.

"Only as old as you feel and as long as the parts keep working, I'll keep going," he says smacking Mom on the ass.

"That's really disturbing to share with your kid you know. Just saying." I shudder and move to the kitchen table.

Mom sets down a pan of lasagna and tray of garlic bread on the table. After dad pulls out her chair and she sits down, she reaches over and grabs my hand.

"It's so good to have you home. Will you say the blessing?" Mom asks.

We join hands and bow our heads. I haven't kept up the tradition of saying grace, and just that word makes her image flash through my thoughts. Clearing my throat and shaking the thoughts away, I begin, "Thank you, heavenly Father, for the chance to be home again. For my parents' continued love for one another and hope for a love like theirs to call my own. Thank you for this wonderful food.

I pray for continued blessing for all of my family. In the name of your son, Jesus Christ, Amen."

"Very nice. I'm taking from the blessing you still don't have anyone of significance in your life?" Mom asks.

I shake my head, not knowing how to even talk about this with them. "I was holding out for someone that, it turns out, I shouldn't have been holding out for. Coming home, it's like nothing has changed, but everything has. That doesn't even make any sense."

"No, it actually does. You grew up, and when that happens, you look at things a whole lot differently than you used to. Everything okay?" Dad asks.

"Yeah, I met with Akia today and I think we resolved a few things. I think I need to feel like everything is okay with you two as well. I feel like I let you down by leaving. It was selfish. I'm sorry if I hurt you."

"Boy, we knew you would be heading out into the world one day. Knew it from a very early age. I'm glad you finally cleared things up with Akia. I think she needed that closure. But to be clear, you didn't hurt us. Sure, we were sad to see you go, but kids leave. It's part of life. There's always a hope that they come home one day, though," he says with a smirk.

I hesitate in my response causing my mom to jump out of her chair. "You're coming home, aren't you?"

"Now, Little One, don't get all excited just yet. You don't want to guilt him into making a decision," Dad interjects.

Mom immediately sits down. I never understood the dynamics of my parent's relationship. It was never abnormal to me growing up. Now as a grown man, it's becomes relatively clear that my mother is submissive. The nickname, the way she immediately responds to my dad, I feel the need to wash my brain of all the thoughts that suddenly come forward. I find myself looking back and forth between them.

"I see the wheels turning. We can discuss that later, if you want. Otherwise, let's continue with this conversation, and close your mouth before you catch flies," Dad quickly says.

There are just some things you never want to discover about your parents. I've just been mentally scarred for life. I'm in shock and just start laughing. I can't help it. My natural reaction to shock used to be anger, but it's been replaced lately with uncontrollable laughter.

"What did I miss?" Mom asks, looking at me with a weird look.

Suddenly it's like a light bulb goes on as her eyes go wide. She joins in with my laughter. "Took you long enough. Damn Zeke, you act like you haven't been around us during your adult years. We hang out at the resort every year for goodness sake."

"Please for the love of all things holy, stop. I'll consider moving back home if you just stop and please change the subject. Can we just eat and pretend none of this ever happened? Please?" I beg.

My dad chuckles, my mom claps her hands excitedly, and I fold my head into my hands.

"Zeke is moving home! This is the best news ever!" My mom giggles, taking a mouthful of lasagna.

Is there such thing as a mental wash? I need a stiff drink after this. I move from closure to horror to that feeling of home as I see the excitement on my Mom's face.

# CHAPTER EIGHT

*Connection*

## ZEKE

I had some seriously screwed up dreams last night. I see that things were not always as they seemed in more ways than just how I viewed my hometown. I wonder if there is anything I over looked with Uncle Chance and Aunt Patience, but I can't seem to come up with anything. They seem as vanilla as they come.

I'm up at the crack of dawn again and follow my same routine as the day before. I'm hoping to see Gracie again. Hopefully I don't scare the shit out of her today. I glanced through my old high school yearbooks after dinner last night, and I do remember her now. She always seemed to be in the background, but I remember Kee paying special attention to her, always trying to make sure she was included.

Gracie has definitely grown up. The only thing I really recognized where those eyes. Although hidden behind glasses, they still stood out in the photos I saw. She is definitely all woman now, with the real life hour glass figure, full breasts, and full hips.

I find myself daydreaming when I spot her walking towards the barn, her pony tail and hips swinging in a synchronized dance. I clear my throat to get her attention before saying good morning.

She returns the greeting and waves but continues to walk into the barn. Well damn. I was just dismissed. That isn't going to fly with me. I realize she is working, but shit. I brew another cup of coffee as I throw on jeans, a clean shirt, and boots.

Jogging down the steps trying not to spill the coffee, I rush to the barn in hopes she didn't take off to somewhere else.

## GRACIE

Can I be any more of a nerd? I knew he was up on the balcony before I heard the clearing of his throat. I had hoped to sneak by without him seeing me. He's so far out of my league, it's not even funny. Of course, he picked up that slow southern drawl. Even his movements appear slow, although that could all be in my head. Like the image I have of him on Zeus. I saw him take off yesterday and it was a beautiful sight. In my image there includes a sunset.

I've never been good around guys. The few boyfriends that I have had were at least approachable. In my league, comfortable and boring. I'm not shy by any means. I can carry on a conversation with normal people. He is anything but normal. He is celestial. The type of guy who can command a room with just a smile. The kind of guy who has skinny girlfriends hanging on their arms. Who probably has that skinny girlfriend waiting for him back in Texas. Pam said he was here alone. Wouldn't he have brought her home with him? Pam acted like she wanted to play matchmaker, but we couldn't be a more uneven pair.

I don't think I'm fat, don't get me wrong, but I'm certainly not skinny. I've never been totally comfortable in my own skin. I try and see what Akia says she sees, but my mirror isn't very friendly to me. *Yes, I blame the mirror.* Once inside the barn, I stop and look down at my body. From this angle and without that lying mirror, I like what I see. I have full perky breasts. I like the way my hands fit on my waist right above my hips. I have great hips and a great set of legs. I even think my feet are cute, and feet are normally gross. Just saying.

"Coffee?"

"Fuck! Would you stop scaring the shit out of me?" I exclaim, spinning around to see a smiling Zeke holding out a mug.

"Damn, girl. You are jumpy in the morning," he says chuckling.

"No, you are just stealth-like or something. Make some damn noise at least," I say, taking the offered mug. "Thank you...for the coffee, not the scare."

"You are welcome. So, I need to apologize," he says.

"Umm, okay? For what?" I ask.

"I didn't recognize you yesterday, and I realize now why you gave me the stink face with my choice of nicknames. I'll have to come up with another one that doesn't cause you to wrinkle up like that."

He knows who I am. Great, or not so great. I'm now lost for words. I start shifting from side to side. I shove the half of coffee back into his chest.

"Thanks for the coffee, I have to...umm...work. I have to work," I say, stumbling over my words.

"Later, Demon Zeke," I say and go to move past him.

I feel a strong arm come gently across the front of my chest, above my breasts, stopping me in my tracks.

"Wait. Have dinner with me tonight." His voice is gentle and almost a whisper. It sends a warm pulse down my body.

"I can't. I promised Pam I'd help her bake deserts for the wedding," I respond in the same hushed tone.

"Thursday night, then. I have to pick up my tux tomorrow night and make sure Doug passes the Z test."

"Z test? Never mind. I can only imagine." I want to say yes, but really, is he being serious?

"Say yes. It's just dinner. You can catch me up on all the gossip I've missed over the years."

Just dinner, is he serious, again? Maybe that's all it really is to him, though. Just dinner. It has to be. I'm reading into this, and I'm only setting myself up for disappointment. Taking a deep breath, I look up and almost lose myself in his deep brown eyes.

"Sure, why not. It's just dinner," I give in.

"Great. I'll be over to pick you up around six, okay?" The smile he gives me has my heart beating faster.

"Six, sure. See you then," I say as he lowers his arm and lets me walk past him.

Shit, what the hell did I just agree to? I haven't been on a date in a long time. But it's not a date, right? It's just dinner. I mentally chastise myself again for reading too much into this.

## ZEKE

I got her to agree to dinner, but somehow, I feel like she didn't really want to go and only agreed because I practically begged her. I don't know what to make of that. I know I didn't imagine that flare in her eyes or the intake of breath. Her response mimicked my hush tone as well.

When I put my arm out to stop her, I was right about her breasts. Barely touching the top, yet I could almost feel how soft they would be.

I decide to go over and help out with the deserts. Maybe I can get a better read on her that way. It's not like I have anything better to do. Spending more time with Gracie, yeah, that sounds really good to me.

I always helped when I was growing up with the lady lock cookies. I can't make the shell for shit, but I can fill them like a champ. If there were a contest, I would win hands down with the most filled in the quickest time.

I didn't realize what I was getting myself into, though. When I walk through the back door, there are cookies and pastries everywhere. Flour on the floor and across every visible space. It appears that I'm the only man present with at least ten women. My mom along with my aunts, and what I'm assuming are the all the bridesmaids, bustling around the kitchen. There's an incredible harmony, which you don't normally expect with so many women in a kitchen. I see Flower sitting at the table, boxing up cookies as the girls bring them over after they have cooled. I don't want to mess up the system they have going, so I quietly take a seat beside Flower and start helping her box up the goodies.

I see her slip a buckeye in her mouth as she winks and puts up a finger to her mouth making the "shhh" face. I start laughing and the whole entire kitchen goes silent and comes to a halt.

My eyes immediately find Gracie's as she says, "See, stealth. Told you."

"Just like his mom, she would show up and scare the crap out of me all the time," Aunt Carrie laughs.

"Yeah, but she's tiny. Zeke is well, not so much," Aunt Patience chimes in.

"Wow, so this is what I've been missing all these years? Being talked about like you aren't even in the room," I joke.

Akia claps her hands and gets everyone's attention. "Let's get back into this, ladies, and leave the poor guy alone. We are in the home stretch. Don't lose focus."

I wink at Gracie and see a slight blush fall across her cheeks. I can't stop watching her as she moves around the kitchen. If anyone could have been named perfect, it would be her. She has a definite grace about her.

Every once in a while, she makes eye contact and that blush flashes back across her cheeks. It's like she's the only one in the room.

I feel a soft hand placed over mine. Flower leans over and whispers, sort of, "Either you did smuggle some of that good weed from Texas and you are really high, or you are smitten."

"Not sure what you mean," I respond.

"Whatever, I may be old there, boy, but I know that look. I've seen it quite a few times over the years."

I smile and shake my head, trying to play dumb. It's definitely lust I'm feeling, that I will at least admit. If it weren't for my mom and other family members being present, I would be struggling to keep myself from getting hard.

After a few hours the kitchen starts to clear until there's only me and Gracie left. Gram Pam retired to bed about an hour ago and the kitchen is almost cleaned. I wanted the opportunity to have some alone time with Gracie, so I volunteered to help finish cleaning. I practically pushed the other girls out the door.

"Impressive lady lock skills you got there, pal," Gracie says, bumping my hip with hers.

"I was born to pump the cream," Realizing how that sounded, I try to back pedal. "That just sounded a bit disturbing, sorry," I laugh.

"Yeah, that was pretty bad. It rivals that devil statement the other day," she says laughing.

"Hey, that's one of my best lines, sweetheart," I joke. "It got you to call me Demon Zeke, though didn't it?"

"Yeah, yeah. You know you didn't have to stay, right? There wasn't a whole lot left, I could have handled it."

"I'm quite enjoying the company, and honestly, didn't want to leave." I bump her back, mimicking what she had done just minutes earlier.

I notice a little bit of flour right under her left ear on her neck. Reaching out, I place my finger softly on the spot and rub it off. She stills immediately, and my eyes flick from her mouth to her eyes. Those eyes quite simply captivate me. I want nothing more than to kiss her right now. I run my other fingers around the back of her neck and place my thumb right on the underside of her jaw.

"You have the most beautiful eyes," I whisper as I watch her eyes flutter closed. "I'm going to kiss you now."

Her eyes immediately flash open, and I'm not sure if I see panic or fire. I don't want to lose the moment, so I quickly lean in and give her a soft closed mouth kiss. The blood rushes straight from my head to my groin and I step away.

"Lips soft too, just like I imagined." I pull her forward and lay a soft kiss on her forehead and mutter against it, "I better go before I get carried away and possibly disrespect my Gram's house."

I hear her sigh and feel her nod against my lips. I force myself to let her go and walk towards the door. Looking back, she has one hand placed where mine was seconds ago and the other pressed against her lips.

"Good night, Gracie. Sweet dreams," I say as I walk out the door.

I hear a soft, "Good night, Demon Zeke."

## GRACIE

I feel his eyes on me the entire evening. I try not to look, but I can't help it. I want to make sure he's actually looking at me and it's not my imagination.

It's not.

I feel myself blushing every time we make eye contact. It's difficult to remain calm with him sitting there looking all gorgeous.

There were several times that someone would be talking to me, and I wouldn't hear a thing they said. I'm instead straining to hear the conversation he is carrying on with Flower. I catch myself laughing out loud at some of the things I overhear. He's so incredibly sweet in his interactions with her.

Before I know it, everyone is gone but me and Zeke. I can feel myself begin to sweat. I tried to get him to leave saying I could finish cleaning up myself, but he refuses.

I'm struggling to find something to say and come up with complimenting him on his lady lock skills. It takes everything in me not to bust out laughing at his response. Instead I take the route to almost criticize his flirting.

When he falls silent and I feel his finger run across my neck, I completely freeze. If I didn't know better, he looks like he's going to kiss me. Why the hell is he looking at me like that, and why the hell would he want to kiss me?

He grabs the back of my neck and compliments my eyes. The sensation of his strong warm fingers and thumb makes my whole body hum. Just as my eyes start to flutter close, he says he's going to kiss me.

My eyes fly open in shock, and before I can do anything, he leans in and presses his lips against mine. It's over before I really have a chance to enjoy it, and I'm still not sure if I imagined it or not.

The gentle kiss he gives me on my forehead seems more significant somehow.

I watch him as he walks out the door and all the way over to the apartment. When he disappears from view, I'm snapped out of my trance.

It was just a kiss and nothing more. Right? I can't over think this, it'll just lead to a broken heart. There's no reason I can't enjoy his company while he's here though. I mean for the next week and a half I'll have the chance to get to know him better and gain a friend. Plus, if I ever want to go to Texas, I'll know someone there.

I go through my routine of getting ready for bed. It's later than I normally like to go to bed, and I know I'm going to be dragging tomorrow.

It's really hot in my bedroom from all the baking that happened today. Pam turns off the central air as soon as the evenings start to cool, but I don't think she thought about the heat from the oven from today.

I take a quick shower and walk over to my bedroom wrapped in a towel. Flipping on the light, the ceiling fan starts spinning. The air starts to instantly cool a bit pulling in the night air from my open windows. I drop my towel and pull on a pair of sleep shorts and a tank top.

Reaching up to pull the chain to turn off the light, my room goes dark. Once my eyes adjust, I see a silhouette in the window from the apartment. Shit, I totally forgot my room faced in that direction. Fuck. Did he see me? How much did he see? Oh my God. If he had any interest in me before, I'm sure it was squashed the moment he saw all of this.

I mentally chastise myself. I hate that these insecurities seem to consume me. I'm beautiful and I know this. Someone will see it one day.

I smile as I crawl into bed. Who knows, maybe Zeke liked what he saw. If he didn't, his loss. I feel a tinge of excitement thinking of him watching me. Hell, this could actually be fun. I could put on a little show every night. Imagining him getting off is a total turn on. An older song pops into my head as I reach under the covers and into my shorts. I find myself completely wet. A give myself a quick orgasm and fall into a deep sleep.

# ZEKE

I can still feel her lips against mine. The flash of her blue eyes has embedded themselves into my brain.

As I'm grabbing my night clothes for a quick shower, I notice a light going on in the main house. I find myself walking to the window. What I see takes my breath away. I shouldn't be looking. This is so wrong, but I can't seem to make myself look away.

The ceiling fan is making the shear curtains move and causing me to almost go into a trance. I'm stunned as I see the towel drop and see her glorious body on full display. She is like a goddess you see in the old time oil paintings. All woman. Full breasts that I can see myself worshiping. Those curves that a woman should have, but so many think aren't sexy, are right in front of me. I wish I could transport myself over there right now.

I have an erection that trumps all erections I've ever had in my life. I can't help but reach down and palm myself through my jeans. I groan as I see her pull on her sleep shorts and then a tank top. To cover up that masterpiece is almost criminal.

The light goes off and I'm still standing here watching, wanting more. Both of our windows are open. I can no longer see her, but I think I hear the rustle of the covers being turned down and her crawling into bed. It may be my imagination, but I think I hear her let out a soft moan. It instantly sends a joint down my spine and straight to my groin. Looks like I will have to take care of things in the shower.

# CHAPTER NINE

*Heart to Hearts*

## ZEKE

Today I get to hang out with the guys in the wedding. We are getting our tuxes and going to dinner and getting drinks. There's quite a crew of us, both young and old. Although the uncles are not actually in the wedding party, Akia wanted them in tuxes.

Uncle Bradley pulled Uncle Bruce into one of the changing rooms after he came out in his tux. I heard Uncle Bradley mumble something like "still delicious" as he shoved him in and closed the door.

I see that nothing has changed over the years. I can remember that two of the three would always seem to disappear when we were together in public. Sometimes it would be all three of them. When I would ask either of my parents where they had gone, I would get the explanation that their love was very strong. They were not always comfortable with showing it in public. So, when any of them would feel the need to express it, they would find somewhere private to do so.

I find it inspirational that love can withstand the test of time. However, being older, I understand what really is going on. Yet, I still feel both grossed out by the fact they are still doing things when they are so old, and encouraged that they still can do things being that old.

They both come back out several minutes later with their tuxes slung over their shoulders. Uncle Bradley has his arm around Uncle Bruce's waist and is smiling ear to ear.

"Been a while since we've done that. Well, we've had our appetizers, let's head out so we can get our main course grub on, boys," Uncle Bradley announces.

There's a sound of a few groans and laughter through the store. As my dad says, "Do you really feel the need to overshare there, bud?"

"Well, yes, I actually do. These boys need to know that even when they get old, there's still hope they won't lose their mojo," Uncle Bradly boasts.

Laughing, Doug slaps Uncle Bruce on the back. "Okay, you two. Our reservations are coming up at the restaurant. We need to head out."

I've been doing a mental tally of positives and negatives on Doug. Even though I'm okay now with Akia getting married, I'm still not sure I'm okay with her marrying Doug. So far, he has all positive tick marks. The fact that he seems so comfortable and acceptable of Uncle Bruce and Uncle Bradley, helps him in the positive category.

Once we get to the restaurant, we are seated in the back at a few tables to accommodate us all. I'm sitting in-between my dad and Uncle Chance.

While talking to the group, I feel an arm come around my shoulder. "So glad you made it home for this. You know how important you are to my girl, right? How are you holding up?" Uncle Chance asks in my ear.

"Um, she means the world to me, too, wouldn't miss it for the world. But why are you asking me how I'm holding up?" I ask.

"Take a quick walk with me, will you?" he asks.

We excuse ourselves from the table and go outside to the enclosed patio.

Uncle Chance clears his throat. "I know how much you care for Akia. I know that she felt like it was her fault that you left the way you did. I want to make sure you are okay with all this. It would kill her if you didn't accept Doug."

"You knew?"

"I think everyone in the family knew, Zeke. It was written all over your face every time you looked at her. Your family has a knack of being able to identify love when we see it," he responds.

"We've cleared that up already, sir. We are good. It wasn't her fault, and even though I love her…I want her to be happy. My love has evolved over the years, you could say. Gram Pam summed it up the other day calling it puppy love. Now, I'm not sure how I feel about Doug. Only because I don't really know him, but he's growing on me," I laugh.

"Good to hear, son. Doug is a good man. He loves my girl and shows her every chance he gets. Believe me. He's been put through the ringer with all the family over the past few years. He's gained each of every one of our respect. He even asked me for my permission to ask her to marry him. I know you have to form your own opinion. But give him a chance, yeah?"

"Yeah, I will and thanks. I appreciate your taking the time to talk to me about this. I feel weird now, though, knowing everyone knew," I say, bowing my head.

"Don't. We didn't. We all thought it was cute, and honestly, I liked knowing you were always looking out for her. Wouldn't have wanted it any other way," Uncle Chance says, pulling me in for a hug. "Let's get back."

I seem to be getting a lot of heart to hearts while I'm home. I'm learning a few things in the process. One thing is predominate: I have a great family who looks out for one another and loves me.

When we get back to the table, Uncle Bradley stands and comes over to ask if he can talk to me.

"Okay, hold on everybody. Uncle Bradley, please sit back down. Listen, it seems like everyone feels the need to have a heart to heart with me tonight, so in order for me to actually get to eat, drink a few beers, and relax, let me just say something. First, Doug I don't want this to be uncomfortable for you. My family all seems to speak of you in high regard. I'd like to form my own opinion, but your happily ever after is just a few days away. I'm sure you already know most of this and it seems my family all knew too."

"Growing up I had told Akia that I was going to marry her. I loved her for as long as I can remember. She didn't feel the same. I was pissed that we were raised to believe we were family and that was the reason she felt we could never be together. Although now I realized it was more about her not having the same feelings, family or not. That wasn't the reason why I left. I always felt like I was being smothered in this small town and I needed to get out there and experience the country."

"Coming home has been an eye opener for me. I realize that my family is simply incredible. That what Mom always said is in fact true. The bond we have goes deeper than blood. I'm okay with all of this, I'm good. I still love Akia, but that love is different. I no longer feel that feeling in my gut like I used to. I want her to be happy, and I know it was never meant to be with me. So please, for the love of God, can we just move along and eat?"

Uncle Bradley starts clapping, "Z-man…great speech. But I was just going to ask if you brought any of the good weed home with you."

"Besides," Uncle Bruce pipes in. "Mom already told us that you have your eyes set on a certain little handler at the farm."

I pull my hat off my head and rub it nervously. "Isn't anything sacred around here?"

Getting a slap on the back from Dad, he says, "Nope. Welcome home, boy."

I finally get to eat my now cold burger and suck down a few beers. The conversation is flowing, and I'm learning more about Doug in the process. I like him. I really do. I also trust my family and they all really like him like he's already a part of us.

# CHAPTER TEN

*Date Night*

## ZEKE

I got home pretty late last night. The first thing I did was go to my window and look over at the main house. The lights were all off. I was disappointed I may have missed another show.

Tonight I get to take her out though. So that makes up for it in a way. I have something special planned. At least, I hope she will think so. I haven't seen her at all today, but it gives me time to get my thoughts together and be prepared.

I have Gram Pam helping me put together a nice picnic dinner. She has a nice wicker basket that closes to put everything into. I pack up one of the four wheelers with a small table and two chairs, some candles, and all the dinnerware that I'll need. I found a few boxes of the small white Christmas lights and head up to the gazebo. There is electric run up there, so I know that I'll be able to plug the lights in. I just hope they work.

After checking that, thankfully, they all work, I string up the lights around the gazebo. I make a quick trip into town to pick up a various array of flowers. If there weren't already a worn path to the gazebo, I would have made one from all the back and forth I've done today. I need this to be perfect. I have this feeling this is going to be a very important date for us. I get this feeling that she doesn't think this is a real date. I need to make sure she understands that it is. I need to get to know her. I need to understand these feelings I'm having myself. I can't stop thinking about her eyes and those sweet lips.

I drive the four wheeler up to the front door of the farm house at about five minutes before six. I'm dressed in a pair of khaki's and a button down shirt. Holding a bouquet of flowers, I feel my palms sweating as I ring the doorbell.

"Such a gentleman," Gram Pam says as she answers the door. "So dashing, too. Come on in. Gracie will be down in a minute. Poor girl is a nervous wreck," she whispers the last part.

"I'm a little nervous myself, Gram Pam," I say, rubbing my hand over my smooth head.

"Just be you and it will be just fine. Plus, this is a really sweet first date. How are you going to top this one? You've set those expectations pretty high there, boy."

"I think she may be worth it. If I do get more dates, I'll just have to come up with something or try to play it off that these only happen for special occasions."

I hear movement from upstairs and when I glance up, I see a vision. I've only seen Gracie wearing a ball cap, and of course her hair wet through the window.

What I'm looking at takes my breath away. Her hair is down and flowing around her shoulders. She's wearing a cute little sundress that hugs hers curves perfectly. She's carrying a sweater, which is good since it may get a little chilly on the hill this evening.

"You look beautiful, Gracie," I stutter. "Shit, I wasn't thinking you would wear a dress…hold on."

"I can change!" I hear her call out as I turn and rush out the door.

"No, just wait, give me a second. You look amazing. Hold on, I'll be right back."

I shove the flowers into Gram's hands and rush out the door and over to the building that houses all the ATV's. I grab the key to the side by side and climb in. I pull it out as fast as I can, causing a cloud of dust to engulf me. I'm coughing as I get back to the front door. Gram Pam and Gracie are both laughing.

"Sorry, let's start this over," I say around another cough. I snag the flowers out of Gram's hands and push them into Gracie's, who is now standing on the front porch.

"Thank you, Zeke, they are beautiful," she says as she lifts them to her nose and takes in a deep breath.

I take her by the hand and lay a gentle kiss to the top. "Ready?"

"Umm…yeah. Where are we going in the side by side?" she laughs.

"You'll see," I simply say as I lead her to the ATV and sit her in the passenger side.

I try to calm my nerves. Dammit, I'm screwing this up already. Why didn't I think she would be wearing a dress? Of course, she would. She looks incredible.

"Zeke, I could have changed, really I didn't know," she says, still smelling the flowers.

"Hell no, it was faster to switch ATV's. Plus, it would be a crime to rob me of looking at those gorgeous legs all evening," I respond.

As we get closer to the gazebo, I hear her let out a sigh. "Oh my God, it's...beautiful. You did this?"

"Only the best for our first date," I respond.

As we pull up, I turn off the engine and look over. "Stay," is all I say.

She doesn't move, so I get out and move to her side. I reach out both of my hands. When she places hers in mine, I lift her up and place a kiss on both knuckles.

I lead her to the gazebo that has a small table and two chairs. I put all the dinner that Gram helped me with there and it looks pretty damn good.

Pulling out her chair, I wait for her to sit and push her in before moving to take my seat that is next to hers. One thing I learned from my dad was to never sit across from the girl you were trying to get to know. Always make sure you sit as close to her as you can.

"So, Gracie. I'd like to get to know you better. Tell me what you have been up to since high school," I say.

I'm feeling a little awkward, and I can sense she's feeling the same. I want this to be natural, but how do I break this tension?

"Well, I originally went to school to be a vet, like Akia. However, I couldn't stomach the dissections. So, I switched to business and now I'm putting my love of animals and my degree in business to good use. At least I hope. William is wonderful to work for and I just love the farm. I don't know my official title. Business manager assistant, maybe. But I love what I'm doing and I love helping Pam."

"Sounds amazing. Enjoying what you do for a living is really important. I love what I do. When I can put away someone for a crime simply by breaking down their computer...nothing better."

"That sound incredible, Zeke." She hesitates and takes a deep breath.

"What are you thinking, Gracie? I see those wheels turning," I ask.

"Zeke? What is this? Really. I need to know. I've never had anyone do this much for me on a date. I'm a little overwhelmed and I'm not sure what's happening here," she puffs out as she tucks her head into her chest.

Reaching out, I lift her face up by her chin. "It's a date. A date with a beautiful woman that I want nothing more than to get to know better. You are the most beautiful woman I've ever met."

"Stop, I don't know what to say. This is incredible, but why me?" she asks.

"Not sure what you mean by that. Why not you? I mean, you are incredibly gorgeous. My Gram Pam loves you and so does everyone else that I've come across that knows you. So, I want to see if you are as beautiful inside as out. Even though I have good instincts and think that you will be. I feel lucky that no one has snatched you up. Do you believe in fate?" I ask.

"I guess...I'm not sure. I'd like to believe," she responds with a smile.

"I believe in being open and honest with everyone that is in my life. I have had some incredible role models in my life that have shown me how special it is to find your person. I could spend all evening telling you the lessons I've learned from them. What I'm getting at is this: I really didn't want to come home. I thought I was in love with Akia. I've had feeling for that girl for as long as I could remember. I really thought having to watch her marry someone else was going to be one of the hardest things in my life." I see Gracie nod her head seemingly knowing the history.

"I waited for that punch in the gut the first night I saw her again in person. It never came. So, I was waiting for something to happen when I hugged her. It never did. For the first time, in a very long time, I felt free. Free of the angst and the bitterness I felt every time I thought about her not feeling the same way about me. The next morning, I wake to the sun in my face, and I was not ready to get out of bed. I'm so glad I did. Because I saw this vision of beauty walking out of the barn like a dream. Then I scared the shit out of her and it makes me laugh each time I think of it," I smile.

"How nice to know the memory of our first meeting is so embarrassing," Gracie says, covering her face.

"Don't be embarrassed. It was cute and something we can tell our kids about one day," I tease.

"Whoa there, buddy. Getting a little ahead of yourself, aren't you?"

"Well, I've been wrong before. I'm teasing you anyways. Please, eat before it goes cold. I will preface by saying it is perfectly safe to eat, since I didn't cook it. Gram Pam helped me in that aspect." Laughing, I motion to the spread of food in front of us.

The conversation flows easily from there and I'm entranced by her sweet voice and animated movements when she talks. We talk about high school and laugh about some of the antics of our classmates. I'm amazed that she was there for many of our hidden tailgate parties. I had no clue she was even there. It kind of makes me mad that I missed out on knowing her back then.

As the sun starts to set, the dimmer switch kicks on and the whole gazebo lights up like a Christmas tree.

"Oh wow. I didn't even notice the lights. So beautiful." Gracie's face lights up and the twinkling causes her eyes to almost glow.

"Yeah...beautiful," I say, staring at her in awe.

## GRACIE

I'm in complete shock. The gazebo is covered in flowers and candles and there's a sweet little table set up with a lot of food on it. He's smooth, I have to hand it to him. He's saying all the right things and making me feel like the luckiest girl in the world. I hate that I'm second guessing him, though. I don't want to, but I'm just in disbelief that he did this for me. Talk about the flutter of butterflies, I have an army in my stomach right now.

Taking a small bite of the piece of cheesecake, I'm stuffed. "This is delicious, but I don't think I can eat another bite, sorry," I say and accidently let out a small burp.

I slam my hand over my mouth and mumble out an 'I'm sorry.'

Zeke laughs as he stretches back and lets out a rumbling size belch. "There. Feel better?"

I bust out laughing, and although I know I shouldn't, it was almost like a challenge. I don't back down from challenges. I mimic Zeke, leaning back and letting out an equaling impressive belch myself.

"Oh, is that how it's going to be. You're on. I can burp with the best of them sweet girl," he says as he starts burping out the alphabet. I'm laughing so hard there are tears streaming down my face.

"Oh my God, stop. I'm going to be sick after eating all this food and laughing so hard. Uncle, I give up. You win!" I say, wiping my eyes.

Zeke pats his chest and lets out on last burp throwing his hands in the air. "Yes. Champion once again."

He stands and starts wrapping up the dishes and putting them into a wicker basket that was sitting on one of the gazebo benches. I see pile of blankets set off to the side. I refill our wine glasses and go over to sit down. I'm trying to be as lady-like as I can, but who am I kidding? I end up sitting on the bench and then sliding to the floor. I tuck my legs beside me and look around proud that I didn't spill anything from the glasses.

"You are one of the most expressional people I've ever seen. I think I could watch you all day," Zeke says as he grabs a guitar I didn't notice leaning against the bench.

"I didn't spill anything. So, no alcohol abuse, which is truly a crime you know," I say laughing.

Zeke sits down beside me with his legs crisscrossed. He starts strumming the guitar and I notice it's an old Daughtry song. I heard that he sang, but holy shit, the boy can sing. He's voice sends tingles down my whole body.

I find myself starting to harmonize on the chorus. I catch myself and stop. Zeke stops playing, causing me to look up at him.

"Why'd you stop? Keep singing. That was amazing,"

I nod my head as he starts back where he left off. I join back in with harmonies as we smile at each other through the entirety of the song.

We end up sing a few more songs together and I find myself snuggling in and leaning my head against his shoulder. When I feel Zeke's lips press against my forehead, I close my eyes and sigh.

I try my best to suppress a yawn, but the harder I try, the harder it becomes.

"It's getting late. As much as I don't want this evening to end, it's going to be a long day tomorrow. We probably should head back," Zeke says, kissing my forehead quickly and standing.

He tells me to stay put and starts grabbing things until his arms are full, putting them into the back of the side by side. I pull a blanket around me and lift myself up onto the bench.

I'm surprised when Zeke comes over and scoops me up into his arms. I cringe a little inside and look to see if there is any sign of strain on his face. He bounces me once like I weigh nothing and walks over placing me gently into the passenger side.

My face must show my shock because Zeke leans down and kisses my nose. "What's with that face? I can tell I'm going to have fun learning all those unique faces you make."

"Oh, um, well. I'm just a little taken back. I mean, I'm not exactly little and you just picked me up like I was a feather," I say, tucking my head.

"You are perfect and felt really good in my arm, by the way. So, I'm not sure I understand what you mean?" he says, moving to the driver's side.

I know he knows exactly what I mean, but again seems to know exactly what to say. I've gone out with guys who have made comments about my weight seemingly to joke but they only made me feel like crap. I'm learning quickly that Zeke is different. He's a gentleman and gentle with his words.

We pull up to the front of the main house and Zeke jumps out, taking me by the hand and walking me up to the door.

"Thank you for tonight. This was the best date I've ever experienced. Not sure how you are going to top this one," I say, pulling the blanket a little tighter around me.

"Thank you for agreeing to go out with me and letting me enjoy your company. You have an amazing voice. Since you seem to be challenging me to top this one, I guess that means I'll have a chance to have a second one?" he says, wrapping me in his arms.

"Well yeah, at least to see if you can top this one of course," I say, looking up at him.

"Good. Because I like you Gracie. You are going to the rehearsal, right? I was planning on taking Gram Pam, so I'd like you to come with us." He's now rocking us back and forth almost like we are dancing.

"Didn't Akia tell you?"

"Tell me what?" he asks, stopping our movements.

"You and I are paired up in the wedding, so yeah I'm going and yes, I would hope we could all go together." I see a smirk come across his face.

"So that's what she meant when she said she hoped you would forgive me for calling you Squeak. My wedding party partner, huh? Damn this trip keeps getting better and better." He chuckles.

Lifting my chin with his fingers, he slowly leans forward and places his lips against mine. Moving his fingers around to the back of my neck, I feel his mouth open, pulling my bottom lip inside. I gasp and he takes the opportunity to give me a kiss that has my whole body on fire.

He stops and pulls back resting his forehead against mine. I reach up and run my fingertips across his beard and let out a deep sigh.

"I better get inside. Thank you again, Zeke," I whisper.

"Yeah, better get yourself inside because I may just lose a little control here," he says kissing my nose.

I watch as he moves to get some of the items from the back of the ATV and I swear I hear him mumble, "Hope I get another show tonight."

"What?"

"What?" he responds with a huge smile and a wink, jogging backwards to the apartment steps.

He stops and motions his head for me to go inside. I walk in and close the door behind me smiling as I jog up the stairs. Oh, I'll give him a show alright.

# ZEKE

Her comment alluding to her weight pissed me off, but I think I played it out okay. She has no clue how beautiful she is, how her body is like a dream land.

To think that Marilyn Monroe would have never been a pin up model by today's standards is just sad. It may seem hypocritical since I work out religiously and my friends joke that my muscles have muscles, yet I find nothing attractive with a women having as many muscles as me. A woman's body is supposed to be soft. Soft enough is sink into and feel it wrap around you. She's like an undiscovered diamond that I plan on digging up and treasuring.

The fact that she seems to be a little kinky has my blood boiling in excitement. I know she heard me, and I pray that she in fact gives me a little show tonight.

Once I see her enter the house and close the door, I rush up the steps and drop the wicker basket on the counter and my guitar on the couch. I switch off the lights and move immediately to the window.

I watch as I see her light go on and the curtains start to move from the fan. I see her glance quickly in my direction and turn her back. Yeah, she knows I'm watching. I can tell because her movements are slow and seductive. I see her slowly grab her dress and pull it over her head. As she drops it to the floor, she lifts her hair and pulls it over her shoulder. Reaching behind her, she releases the clasps of her bra, shimmying her shoulders and letting it drop. Walking to her dresser, her hips move from side to side, and I immediately undo the button and zipper of my pants.

She bends over rubbing her legs together like she's trying to get friction to her core. Reaching down, she pulls out a pair of sleep shorts as I reach down and release myself from my pants.

*Turn around, turn around*, I'm chanting in my head, but she doesn't. She continues to tease by setting the shorts on her dresser and slowly peeling her lacy underwear over her hips until they slip down her legs to the floor.

Christ, it's almost like I can see her glistening from her wetness between her legs. She spreads her legs slightly as her hand moved down between them. I can see her fingers as she slides them through the gap in her legs.

I fist my erection and give it a tug feeling a jolt right in my balls. Rubbing my thumb through the pre-cum, I place my palm against the window and spread my legs.

I let out a growl and notice that Gracie turns her head to the side and smiles like she heard me. I see as she raises the hand that was just between her legs and slowly put them into her mouth. Her eyes flutter closed as she sucks on them.

I increase the speed of my strokes feeling that familiar tingle down my spine. Gracie moves slightly to the side so I can see her pinch her nipple as her other hand goes back down between her legs.

I let out a louder than I want "*Fuck*" as she arches her back and I see her arm start to move faster and faster. I can't really see what she is doing, but I can image it. I know she must be rubbing her clit as she massages and pinches that nipple that is still on full display. Her head is still turned to the side, her eyes are closed and her lips are open as I see her gasping out breaths.

What comes next has me emptying everything in me against the screen in a rush of ecstasy. Gracie slaps her hand down on the dresser and bends her knees as I see her whole body shake. She lets out the most incredible moan as an orgasm rushes through her.

I'm panting and sweating at the incredible feeling that I just experienced. I place both palms on the window frame and watch as she stands and pulls her sleep shorts on. A tank goes on quickly after and the light goes off.

It may be my imagination, but I swear I hear a "Goodnight Zeke" uttered as the light goes off.

# CHAPTER ELEVEN

*Happily Ever After*

## ZEKE

When I go over to the farm house the next day, Gram Pam is more energetic than normal. She says that she is so excited to see this union and so excited to hear about my date with Gracie.

I tell her an enough that has her bouncing in her seat. Giving me a fist pump that I find really sweet, I ask where Gracie is.

"Oh, she'll be down in a minute. That girl usually doesn't take much time to get ready. Lately though, she's been taking forever." She gives me a knowing look.

I hear movement on the steps, so I help Gram Pam up and walk her over to the front door.

"Wow, you look fantastic. All the guys are going to be jealous watching me walk in with the two of the most beautiful ladies in the world," I say.

Gracie smiles but doesn't meet my eyes. There's a slight blush to her cheeks. She wasn't shy last night that's for sure. I don't want to embarrass her and possibly have her second guess the show she gave me. Plus, I want more.

I get them settled into Gracie's car. I wasn't sure if Gram would have been able to get up into the truck. She takes the backseat and Gracie hands me her keys as I get her into the front passenger seat.

I decided on wearing a suit, and I feel like I'm in a strait jacket. It's tailored but still feels constricting. Gracie is wearing a pretty black lace type dress that has a bright blue sash tied around her waist. It almost matches the color of her eyes. She really does take my breath away. She's wearing her hair down again and it has these huge curls that make me want to wrap my fingers around.

I reach out and grab her hand as I head down the road to the church. She intertwines her fingers in mine and give them a squeeze. I quickly glance over and smile. She smiles back at me but slightly hiding behind her hair.

I squeeze her fingers back and pull her hand up to my lips and give them a soft kiss.

"You two sure make a cute couple, you know. Absolutely perfect," Gram Pam pipes up from the back seat.

I look in the rearview and see her nodding her head and smiling. Gracie squeezes her fingers and hand out of my grip and folds her hands on her lap.

The loss of her touch affects me more than it should. It doesn't escape me that she let go after Gram Pam's words.

"Don't know if we are a couple just yet, Gram Pam. I sure wouldn't mind it though," I say, looking back at her in the rearview.

I see Gracie shift in her seat beside me, but she doesn't say a word. She hasn't spoken a word this whole time.

We make it to the church and Gracie jumps out and helps Gram, walking ahead and into the church. Looks like we're going to have to have a talk to see what is going on in her head.

We do a walkthrough of the ceremony with the wedding coordinator directing us on where we should go and where we should stand. I'm trying to pay attention, but I keep trying to get Gracie to look at me. She seems natural, talking and joking with the girls, but I see there's a stiffness to her movements whenever I get close. We take our final walk down the aisle, and I tuck Gracie's hand around my arm, not letting go of her hand.

As we are all standing around the lobby of the church, I try to slip my arm around Gracie's waist, but she pulls away saying she has to get Pam.

Everything seems to go in slow motion as the group heads out to their vehicles to go to the restaurant for dinner. I'm starting to get pissed by the blatant dismissal of Gracie. *What the fuck did I do?*

When we get to the restaurant, I'm glad to see Uncle Bruce waiting on the curb to help with his mom. Gracie tries to get out of the car, but I lean over and pull the door back closed.

The car is uncomfortably silent as I drive around the back to the parking lot.

"What's going on, Gracie?" I ask as I pull in a spot and turn off the engine.

"What do you mean?" she asks with her head tucked.

"Look at me," I state. "Please, Gracie, will you at least fucking look at me, dammit?"

She lets out a deep breath, shifts in her seat, and slowly looks up at me. Her eyes look a little glassy, like she might start crying.

"What is it? Please talk to me and tell me why the hell you look like you could bust out crying any minute. Did I do something?"

"No...it's just all this wedding stuff. It makes girls a little emotional," she says, looking down at her hands.

I quickly shift in my seat to face her and throw my arm up on her headrest. "I'm calling bullshit here. You haven't been able to look me in the eye for more than a second at best all evening. Is this about last night? You act like you are ashamed and you have nothing to be ashamed of darling. That was the most erotic thing I've ever seen in my life."

"Yes...no...I don't know, Zeke. It's last night, it's the wedding, it's Pam's comment about us being a couple. It's everything. I'm feeling a little overwhelmed, and I don't know how to act around you. I don't know what this is between us. Honestly, I'm scared," she says, wiping away a tear that starts to fall.

"Scared about what?" I ask as I reach out and twirl my finger around one of her curls. I watch as the setting sun casts a glow on the strands as they move around.

"I'm scared about what the hell this is between us. I'm afraid of thinking it's more than it is. You're leaving in a week, Zeke. I don't want to start caring about you, then have my heart ripped out as I watch you leave. And I'm scared that I shouldn't be even worrying about all that when we hardly know each other."

"I don't know what this is between us either, but I feel something. I know what I would like it to be. Yes, I'm leaving in a week, but can we just forget about that and let things just happen? Face that when the end of my time here comes?"

"That's just it, though. What if I do start to care about you? Long distance never works. This was over before it even began, really. If it even started to begin with. God, I'm rambling again."

"I like it when you ramble. Listen, give me a chance to get to know you. There are never any guarantees in life. But if there is any chance of this working out, I want to find out. I don't want an invisible barrier keeping us from finding out what this could be. Maybe you will be the reason I come back home, for good." I soften my tone on the last sentence. Feeling a lump form in my throat at the possibilities of what I am saying, I know I can't make any promises, especially that big, but I can't let her give up just yet.

"You can't say or make those kinds of promises, Zeke. At least not yet," she says.

"I can promise I'll be home for the holidays. They aren't that far away. I can promise that if this becomes something, I'll send you a plane ticket to get you away from the snow and enjoy the San Antonio winter."

I lean in to kiss her temple just as banging on the roof starts. "Z-man, stop trying to get to second base and get your ass inside. We are waiting for you dude," I hear Uncle Bradley yell from outside of the car.

Gracie covers her face with her hands and mutters oh God as I let out a small chuckle. I kiss her temple quickly and we both exit the car. She doesn't seem to want me to be a gentleman, and I can deal with that, for now at least.

I open my arms and Gracie complies by walking into them. I tuck her under my arm as we walk into the restaurant. She fits perfectly. I smile as I feel her arm slide around my waist and place her other hand on my stomach.

No one seems to be surprised at how we enter the back room where the dinner is taking place. I'm grateful nobody makes a big deal over it.

I pull her chair out and get her situated as I sit down next to her. I have my arm around the back of her chair the whole evening, playing with her curls every chance I get.

She seems more relaxed now, even leaning into me every once in a while. I see my mom and dad looking at me with smiles on their faces. Being here with family feels right. Being here with Gracie feels even better.

The future bride and groom take off. Kee and her bridesmaids are staying at Gram Pam's, so Pam gets a ride back with Kee. Some of us decide to stay a little longer heading, out to the bar for a few drinks.

As we are standing around one of the high tops, I see one of my high school friends, Eric, walking toward us.

"Zeke, is that you? Damn boy, you beefed up since school, man," Eric says, slapping me on the back.

"Hey Eric, how you been?" I ask.

"Good man. Married with kids and living the dream. What about you? You got anyone down in Texas? That's where you are now, right?"

"That's where I am and nope. But with any luck, I may have someone in my life soon," I say, throwing my arm around Gracie's shoulder.

"Holy shit, Gracie Lynn? Looks like you beefed up too," Eric says, laughing.

I instantly see red. "Apologize now," I say getting in his face.

"You aren't being serious, are you? I mean look at you. You could have any girl you'd want, dude."

"*Dude.* I couldn't be more serious, and you need to apologize. I would count my blessing and be the luckiest man in the world to call that beautiful woman right there mine. Now again, you need to apologize." I'm trying to remain calm but I can feel the veins in my temples start to pulsate.

Eric throws up his hands in defense and lets out a nervous laugh, "Okay, if you say so, calm down man. Gracie Lynn, accept my apologies. I've had a few too many it seems."

He shakes his head, still laughing and walks away. I feel like I could punch something when I feel a soft hand on my back. I instantly feel myself start to calm.

I turn around and see Gracie with a huge smile on her face.

"Why are you smiling, beautiful girl?" I say finding myself returning her smile.

"That was the sweetest thing ever. My knight in shining armor defending his queen," she laughs.

"Got that right, my queen. Never forget it. When did he turn into such a jackass?"

"He's always been an ass. Not everyone from school grew up…guys or girls. I'm used to it, anyways. I've changed a lot and when people realize who I am, they are shocked. Most are nicer than that, though. It's okay," she says, reaching up and rubbing my temple.

"They are finally starting to go away. Damn, those veins were popping."

"It's not okay, Gracie. No one should talk to anyone like that. You are all woman, and I can't tell you how beautiful you are," I say, pulling her in for a hug.

She presses her face into my neck and sighs. "Thank you. I know I'm beautiful. I have no issues with how I look. I just know that some people are superficial. Hearing someone else acknowledge it is a pretty amazing feeling. I think they are just jealous of all this"

"Damn straight. No one in this room, hell this whole city, can hold a candle to what I'm holding in my arms right now."

## GRACIE

I was a little ashamed of what I did last night. There's something about the way Zeke seems to break down my inhibitions. I try to avoid him the best I can, but he doesn't let me in the end.

I end up telling him more that I wanted to, but it was all the truth. I'm scared. I'm having these feelings that I shouldn't be having this soon. When he stood up for me, he pushed himself further into my heart. To finally have someone see you as you see yourself is amazing. I still have a hard time believing this is all happening, but I agree with him in giving this a try. He's right. He'll be home for the holidays and who knows. If anything, it will be a fun fling. I mean, seriously the man is gorgeous. I would be dumb not taking a little advantage of the situation.

Most importantly, I've never had a man look at me the way Zeke does. One look with those sweet brown eyes has me humming from head to toe.

I laugh as we pull up the driveway, and I see faces in the front window looking at us.

"We have an audience. Do you want to give them a show?" Zeke says, pulling me up out of the car.

"Not like the one's I give you. Those are for your eyes only. But hell yeah. Kiss me," I say, pushing him against the car.

"I like a girl who can take charge," Zeke says, grabbing my neck and pulling me in.

He goes all in, like he has never done before. The way he savors my lips is nothing less than incredible. I feel his hardness grinding against my stomach. I reach down and rub him through his pants.

"Christ, Gracie. That feels good, but we have to stop. We are moving out of PG really quickly," he says, pressing himself into my hand.

I move my hand up his chest and around his neck. I kiss his lips, his nose, and then pull him down to kiss his forehead. "I didn't think you could top our first date, and even though this may not have been our second, you topped it tonight. Thank you."

"Sweet! I didn't even have to try. Good night, Gracie. Sweet dreams," he says, pressing his lips against my neck.

"Good night, Zeke," I say as I head up to the house with an extra pep to my step.

When I enter the house, I'm greeted by a bunch of whoops and cheers. Laughing, I raise my fist in the air. I run up the stairs and change in the bathroom. There will be no show tonight. Once I get to my bedroom, I see Akia standing by the bed pulling back the covers.

"I'm sleeping with you tonight. I hope you don't mind. The girls all decided to crash downstairs but thought I should be in a bed. Sometimes being the bride has it's privileges," she laughs as she crawls into bed.

"I snore, just saying. You've been warned," I say laughing.

"So, Zeke, huh?"

"I guess so, keep your voice down. He's probably over there eavesdropping," I say, looking out the window to the apartment.

Akia laughs and snuggles under the covers. "Yeah, just like Zeke. He's a good guy you know," she whispers.

"Yeah, I'm seeing that. I'm surprised though," I say whispering myself.

"Surprised, how?" she asks.

"Why you two never got together. I mean he can be pretty persistent," I say, turning off the lights and crawling under the covers.

"Yeah, he can. But he was always just Zeke to me. It hurt me that I hurt him, but I knew that it would never work. I knew Doug was the one almost instantly. The way he looks at me, how a simple touch can make my body hum, and even way he sometimes says my name. It's pretty incredible," Akia says with a smile.

"I'm so happy for you, Akia. Doug is pretty incredible," I say, crawling in bed.

"Yeah, he is. I think you and Zee make a really cute couple, you know."

"He seems so out of my league, but I can't deny the way he makes me feel. Which scares the crap out of me...just saying," I respond.

"You don't have to tell me why. He's leaving in a week and you are afraid this is just fling. I can see how he looks at you, though. Maybe you'll be the reason he moves home. You would be the most favorite person in this family, that's for sure, no pressure," she laughs.

"Thanks a lot, Akia. Now I have that weighing over my head," I say, burying my head under a pillow.

## ZEKE

Tonight was emotionally draining. I can understand Gracie's concerns, but I really want to explore these feelings. I'm a true believer in living in the moment, but I also know you can't forget about the future. I think I was able to make her see this thing between us should be explored. Then the whole incident with Eric happened. My control over my short fuse was tested that's for sure. I could have laid him out, but, somehow, I managed to keep my fists in check.

There are little signs that keep popping up concerning my feelings for Gracie, from the need to know what's going on in her head, to the need to defend her and the sense of calm I felt from her simple hand on my back.

Reminiscing the evening's events, I'm lying in bed listening to the chirping of the crickets. I almost forgot how quiet it is here compared to the noise of the city. Although the chirping can grain on my nerves, it's peaceful. I would never sleep with my windows open at the condo back in Texas. The fresh evening air is calming. I could get used to this again.

*Wait. Did I just think that?*

I have a life in Texas. A great condo. A fantastic job that I love. If this would work out with Gracie, she could move down there with me. I mean, what does she have here? I know of a bunch of ranches that she could work at, if this is what she wants to do. She has a business degree. She can find work anywhere.

Now I sound like a girl planning out our whole future together. *Get your head in the game and not on the prize.* Even though it's a hell of a prize, this sure isn't a game to me. I think I'm in it to win it.

I wake up the next morning starving, but I don't think it's a good idea to go over and eat at the house. Even though I know damn well Gram Pam has a feast over there. I'm not sure I can handle all the female hormones.

I'm sure there are wedding day jitters and excitement on a level I'll be uncomfortable with. I look in my fridge and see I have stuff to make a few eggs or maybe a very nice large omelet.

I pull out some lunch meat, ham, and bacon along with the eggs and vegetables and get to cooking. I'm a bachelor and I'm pretty good in the kitchen, at least with breakfast food. I can eat that for all three meals if I have to.

I have everything in the pan when I hear a soft knock on the door. Not wanting to burn my omelet, I yell that the door is open.

I hear footsteps and glance over my shoulder to see Gracie in a robe with curlers in her hair.

Chuckling, I say, "Good morning, sexy. Love the curlers."

"All part of the beautification process. Pam sent me over to get you for breakfast, but it appears I'm too late," she says, lifting her curlers and making a pouty face.

The fact that she came over looking like this doesn't escape me. Either she is very confident and comfortable with me seeing her in anyway or she doesn't care. Both can be a good sign or a bad sign. I'm trying to stay positive and say it's a good sign. Regardless it's another thing that pulls at my heart.

"I wasn't sure that I wanted to expose myself to all that hormonal wedding shit. I decided to just cook. Have you eaten? I have plenty to share. If you want to join me that is," I say, continuing to tend to the omelet.

"It smells delicious. Pam made a spread, but the girls seem to be diving in pretty hard. There may not be anything left by the time we got back there, anyways. Are you sure you don't mind?"

"Not at all. Pull up a seat. It'll be ready in a few. I'm planning on adding cheese, if you don't mind?"

"You make it the way you like it. I'll just sit here and enjoy the view. I can't stay too long though, these curlers need to come out soon or I'll look like Shirley Temple," she says, taking a seat at the table.

I add cheese and cut the omelet in half. I grab two plates and two forks and get it plated. I bring the plates over to the table and set one plate in front of her. Handing her a fork, I take a seat and grab her hand.

"This is going to sound weird, maybe, but it's a bit of a family custom to say a prayer when you eat at the table. My dad insisted on it and it's just something that I've always done," I say, bowing my head.

I watch as she smiles and tucks her head into her chest squeezing my hand. "Can I say it?"

And there she goes again, pinging the old heart muscle. I get a lump in my throat. I feel like a damn pussy but damn she knows just what to do and say.

I swallow and nod my head knowing I couldn't say anything right now.

"Thank you, Lord, for allowing me to have the opportunity to have breakfast with Zeke. Thank you for bringing him home to share in this wonderful occasion of seeing Akia get married. It means the world to her that he is here," she pauses and gives me a one-eyed glance and smile. "Bless this food that we are about to partake of. In the name of your son, Jesus Christ, Amen." She squeezes my hand one more time and clears her throat.

"Well done, thank you," I say. I know she probably doesn't know how much that truly meant to me.

Her first bite causes a moan that jolts me straight to my groin. I try to adjust my chair so I can cover my growing erection.

"Oh my God, Zeke. This is incredible," she says, rolling her eyes.

The images that shoot through my brain are anything but innocent. I picture her making that face and moaning while I'm deep inside her. Christ, it's just breakfast and I'm rock hard. I try to say something to get my mind off of my uncomfortable predicament.

"So...how are the girls holding up over there?"

"As good as can be expected...I guess," she laughs. "Akia is buzzing and ready to get this day over."

"Well, I for one can't wait to see the finished product of you. Seriously, you could throw on your dress and go just as you are. You are incredibly beautiful. I'm going to be honored to have you on my arm today," I say, reaching out and running my fingers down her cheek.

She leans into my hand and closes her eyes. "Dammit, Zeke. I'm the one honored that you can look at me like this and still say those words. Okay, I hate to leave you with a mess, but I need to go. These curlers need to come out like now."

"I would have had to clean up anyways. Thank you for joining me. I'm looking forward to seeing you later. Go..."

She jumps up and leans over placing a soft kiss on my cheek. Rushing out the door, she says a happy sounding goodbye. I hear the door click and I place my hands on my head. I'm a goner.

## GRACIE

I'm sitting in the living room having curlers put in my hair. I've never had this done before and not sure why I'm subjecting myself to this now.

Pam comes in and asks if I'll go over and invite Zeke over for breakfast. *Really?* I'm in curlers and a robe. I look at Akia in hopes that she will save me, but she just shrugs her shoulders and laughs.

*Bitch.* Okay, I'm doing it. If he can get over seeing me like this, maybe he is worth investing my time in. This is a test of all tests here. I'm not one to shy away from a challenge. Besides, I can look pretty scary at times. I really like him. I mean I really, really like him. I need to know this isn't a fling for him. I don't like playing games, but I just need assurance that this is actually something that could be something.

I stand up and square my shoulders. "Well ladies, if he accepts me like this, he may just be a keeper."

Akia laughs and says, "Oh girl, he is a keeper. You are just the one to snag him. You may be in curlers and a robe, but I bet a million dollars he doesn't blink an eye at that."

Shit if she wasn't right. He complimented me the moment I walked through the door. He continued to make me feel like I wasn't in a robe and curlers the whole time I was there. If I'm not mistaken, he was even a bit turned on by it all.

I could see him becoming emotional while I was saying the prayer. It took everything in me to keep calm and not get emotional myself. He seriously is amazing. I bet he's broken a lot of hearts over the years, and I bet he's felt bad about each and every one.

I'm pretty excited to see him in a tux. I still can't believe Akia paired me up with him. I wonder if she had something planned all along. I wouldn't put it passed her.

We are all dressed, and I can't believe how good my hair turned out. I don't normally wear a lot of makeup, so I didn't want anything overboard done. The girl that was doing our hair and makeup did a great job at keeping me looking natural, but man did she make my eyes pop.

I love that Akia let us pick out our type of dress. We are all in the same color and length, just all different styles. The color is soft lilac and makes me feel feminine with the lace bodice and flowing chiffon skirt that just reaches my toes. With a pair of simple strap heeled sandals, I feel like I want to go out to the field and just spin while watching the skirt flow out. It reminds me of my first Easter dress that I wouldn't stop twirling in. I think I wore that dress every chance I got.

We all pile into the limo and head over to the church. Akia looks amazing and the glow around her is almost mesmerizing.

# ZEKE

"Is this pink or purple? What the fuck is up with this color dude?" Doug's best man, Jared, complains as he looks down at his tie.

"It's lilac," Doug says shaking his head.

"What's lilac and how do you know what color lilac is?" Jared says, still turning the tie back and forth like it'll change color miraculously.

"It's Akia's favorite color. I like it. Stop being a pussy and complaining," Doug says, hitting the tie out of Jared's hand.

"Of course, you like it. You have to like it. I don't have to like it," Jared says, playing with the tie again.

"But you have to wear it. You can take it off once the pictures are done and we are at the reception. Quit cussing, we are in a church." Doug leans around Jared to me and says, "You want to switch places with him and be my best man? At least you have the decency to stand here and be quiet."

I chuckle and say, "Nah, I don't want to lose who I'm paired up with, but thanks for the offer."

We are standing in the front waiting for the music to start. I hear the preacher clear his throat, and I laugh at how Jared goes rigid straight at the sound.

I can't take my eyes off of Gracie as soon as I see her. All the people simply disappear. Once her eyes meet mine, they never lose contact the whole way up the aisle. Her hair flows over her shoulders in long curls, even softer looking than last night.

She breaks eye contact when she turns left to take her place on the opposite side of the church. With the eye contact broken, my mother comes into full few sitting near the front on the bride's side. She's looking between me and Gracie with a huge smile on her face. She touches a hand to her heart and gives me a quick thumbs up. I shake my hand and laugh at her antics.

I see Gracie is looking at my mom as well but with a face more of panic than humor. When she meets my eyes again, I give her a wink and a smirk that brings a smile back to her face.

I can't even tell you what Akia looked like. I can't even begin to remember anything at all that happened. I never take my eyes off of Gracie the entire ceremony. When I finally meet her at the middle of the aisle, I take a deep breath and let a feeling of utter calm fall around me. I jut out my elbow and pull her hand and arm through mine. Placing my hand over hers, we walk down the aisle together. In my mind the color of her dress changes to white, and I know I'm done. I think it's time to talk to my dad and get some advice on what I'm supposed to do now. I think I know, but I need his intuitive expertise.

# CHAPTER TWELVE

*Departure*

## ZEKE

I'm standing in the middle of the apartment holding a sobbing Gracie tightly in my arms. It's killing me I have to leave her. The week after the wedding flew by so fast. Every moment I had I tried to spend with her.

The evenings at the gazebo were my favorite. We would ride horses up and watch the sunset together. Sometimes we would sing, sometimes we would talk, and sometimes we would just sit in silence. We always took the same position. Me with my back against a post and Gracie between my legs, resting against my chest.

We never made it past kissing. Although the kissing got pretty heated, one of us would always slow it down. It's weird, but I felt like if we had sex, it would somehow taint what we are building. Believe me, I feel sex is very important in a relationship. It creates a strong bond between two people. However, I don't want this to be looked at as just a chance to get down her pants.

"I hate to see you cry, my sweet girl. I'm going to miss you so bad, can you give me a smile please? I don't want the last image in my head to be of your tears until I see you again," I say, leaning back and using my thumbs to wipe the tears from her cheeks.

She gives me a weak smile in return. Dipping down, I lift her face in my hands and press our noses together.

"Before you know it, it'll be Thanksgiving and we'll be together again, yeah?" I feel her nod her head and sniff.

"So, you are planning to come home then?" she asks.

"Couldn't keep me away. I already booked my flight and requested the time off from work. I'll be back the Tuesday before and plan on staying until the Monday after. I'd love for you to come visit me. Any chance you can get some time off work? I'll pay for the flight," I ask.

"Wait, you already bought your ticket for Thanksgiving? Why didn't you tell me? Do you really want me to come visit you or are you just saying that to make me feel better? I never take time off. We start to slow down in October. I can afford my own plane ticket, Zeke. Oh my God, I'm rambling like an idiot."

"But you are no longer crying and that gorgeous smile is back on your face. Besides, I kinda love it when you ramble," I say, pulling her back into my arm and tucking her head against my neck.

I feel her sink into my arms and let out a deep breath. "Okay, I feel better, a little. I'm still going to miss you terribly, but now at least I have something to look forward to,"

"Let me look at my schedule when I get back. I may only be able to take a few days off, but if you come down on a Friday and leave the following Sunday, that will be almost two full weekends. Plus, we'll have every single night together. All night together," I finish in a deeper tone, almost a growl.

"Mmmm, even more to look forward to," Gracie says, kissing my neck.

"Keep that up sweet girl and I'll miss my flight," I say, kissing her forehead just as I hear a knock at the door.

"My evil plans to keep you here have been foiled," Gracie says.

"It's open," I say reluctantly.

My mom and dad walk in, and my mom stops, noticing us in an embrace. "Sorry, Zeke. Hi Gracie, we didn't mean to interrupt."

"It's okay, Mom. I think we are good, right, Gracie?"

"Yeah, I think we are good," Gracie says, tapping my chest and taking a step back.

"You ready, boy? We need to get on the road. Gracie, are you coming with us?" my dad asks.

"I want to, but I can't. Call me when you land. I'll see you soon," she says, giving me a kiss on the cheek, backing away, and rushing out of the door.

My mom tries to stop her, but Gracie dodges her. "Zeke, is she going to be okay?"

"Yeah, if I have anything to do with it, she will. She may not know it yet, but it'll be all good," I respond.

I'm more apprehensive about getting on the plane than I was about coming here. The only thing keeping me going is knowing the plans I have set in motion. I hated lying to her about coming home for Thanksgiving, but I hope the end result will make up for it. I just need to get her down to Texas sometime in October and my plan will hopefully play out the way I want.

On the plane, I purchase the Wi-Fi package and sent off a video message to Gracie.

"Hey, sweet girl. I'm in flight and was thinking about you. Miss you already. Please tell me you will look into coming down to visit me in October. I'll make it worth your while, promise. Anyway, I'll call when I land. Hope you are having a good day. Talk soon." I hit the end video and send it to her with a smile on my face.

Gracie may be clueless but I have several people in on the plan. I just hope that plan doesn't blow up in my face.

# GRACIE

I decide to go ahead and clean up the apartment to keep my mind off of Zeke. Of course, it doesn't exactly work, since this is where he slept. The smell of his cologne engulfs me. There's not much to clean. Zeke did a good job of cleaning up after himself. The bed is even made. I brought over a laundry basket to put in the dirty sheets and towels, so I start to dissemble the bed. As I peel back the comforter, his smell becomes stronger. I just want to crawl in the bed and pretend he's here with me.

My phone buzzes in my pocket. I take it out and smile when I see it's a text from Zeke. When I open it, I see that it has a video attached. Hearing his voice sends the usual tingles down my spine. That smirk of his is adorable, too.

I'm not sure how to respond, so I just send back a smiley face with hearts with eyes. I lift a pillow to take off the case and a piece of folded paper drops to the bed.

When I open it, I see it's a note from Zeke.

Gracie,
I sprayed this pillow case with some of my cologne. Put it on your pillow and think about me when you lay your head on it every night. I'm counting down the days to I'll see you again.
Anyway, miss you sweet girl. Talk soon.
Yours,
Zeke

I get a lump in my throat as I pull the pillow case up to my nose. I end up finding several more notes stuck around the apartment in various places. Each one is as sweet as the last.

I finish up and head over to the main house. As I'm getting ready for bed, Zeke calls. We end up talking for almost an hour. I tell him I'm going to look at booking a flight for the last week of October. Halloween in San Antonio sounds fun. We hang up, and I rest my head on my Zeke pillow and fall quickly to sleep.

## ZEKE

The end of October is perfect. It gives me time to make sure I have everything done and ready.

I call my dad and tell him we have until the end of October. He laughs and says that shouldn't be a problem. He already has the wheels in motion for me. I can't wait for Gracie to get here. She's going to be surprised and hopefully happy.

Work tomorrow is going to be interesting. I've already given them the heads up, but I'm sure I'm going to have a lot of things to attend to in order to make this a reality.

# CHAPTER THIRTEEN

## *Surprise*

### ZEKE

I'm standing at the baggage terminal waiting to see Gracie come down the escalator. I'm fucking nervous. She's going to be in my territory. In my condo. Hopefully in my bed. Our first time together. I'm getting hard just thinking about it.

Plus, there is the whole fact of where this is going to end up. With any luck in the direction I want it to.

I'm trying not to pace. I look up and see her smiling face. When she reaches the bottom of the escalator, she takes off running. I square myself for the impact. Once she is in my arms, I know I've made the right decision. I lift her up as she wraps her legs around me. My hands grab her ass, and oh, what an ass it is. Feeling her press her lips against mine is even more incredible.

We grab her bags and head out to my truck.

"Got some things planned for this week. Most of which will be a surprise. I got the week off of work, so I'm all yours," I say as we head to my condo.

"Oh wow, that's great. I'm so excited. I've missed you," Gracie says, grabbing my hand.

"Missed you, too, sweet girl," I say, pressing her hand against my lips.

We get to my condo and I look for her reaction as we enter.

"This is nice, but Zeke, I expected a bachelor's pad, but where is your furniture?" she says looking around at the mostly empty space.

"Part of the surprise. Let's say I'm renovating," I respond. "I still have obligations at the resort tonight. I hope you don't mind. I want you to be prepared. I'm not sure if you have been told about this resort, but just about everything goes. It's really refreshing actually and has been my connection to my family over the years."

"I've been told a little, and I am intrigued. I think it will be fun. Can I get freshened up and changed before we go?" she asks.

I walk her to my bedroom and show her the bathroom, pulling her luggage as we go. Having her in my personal space is doing something to me.

She walks out in a little sundress and sweater. She's wearing a cute pair of cowboy boots causing dirty images to go through my head.

It's still pretty warm here. So, I'm in a pair of cargo shorts and my standard issue resort polo. I grab my ID card and my rubber bracelet. Gracie glances at the bracelet with a questionable look.

You see, different colors mean different things at this resort. Green means that pretty much anything goes. Yellow is that you are curious and open, and red means you are in a committed and closed relationship.

Putting it on my wrist, I smirk.

"Yeah, well, we'll get you one when we get there. Let's just say it's a requirement even as an employee," I say.

"I've been clued in on those, so I guess I'm going to say…should I be surprised it's yellow?" she says, shifting on her feet.

She looks a little upset. I walk up to her and lift her chin looking into her eyes.

"I'm required to wear one. That does not mean I'm required to do anything. I haven't had a chance to exchange it for a red one. I haven't played there in a while. Also, I haven't been with anyone since before I was back home," I say, searching her eyes.

"It's not really any of my business, Zeke," she whispers.

Taking a step back, I'm trying to respond calmly. "It definitely is your business, Gracie. I'm not sure what you think this is between us, but I'm pretty fucking serious about you."

Gracie steps back into my space and places her hand on my chest. "I'm sorry. I didn't mean to upset you. I guess I didn't want to assume what this is, but I feel the same. Honestly, I guess I was just shocked and jealous when I saw the color of your bracelet and didn't know how to react. Poorly, obviously"

"Jealous, huh?" I say giving her a soft kiss on the lips. "Nothing to be jealous of, sweet girl. I never want to upset you, and I'm sorry that I did."

"It's alright, I'm alright," she says with a smile. "Just a misunderstanding."

"You look adorable, by the way. I'm definitely putting a red bracelet on you the minute we walk through that door," I say, grabbing her hand and spinning her around.

"Now who's acting jealous?" she says laughing.

## GRACIE

I'm so nervous about seeing Zeke again. I went out and bought new bras and underwear for the trip. I could be wrong, but I'm pretty sure we are going to have sex. I tend to overanalyze things and have been stressing out the past few days to prepare. The intimate grooming was my least favorite. I had let that go for a while and it needed some work.

The plane trip was faster than I thought. It didn't leave me much time to mentally prepare. All thoughts of worry left me the moment I saw him standing by the baggage carousel. I took off running and jumped into his arms. It still surprises me that he doesn't struggle to hold me. Any doubt I had left me on how I feel about this man. My only doubt is how he feels.

When we stepped into his condo, I was shocked at how barren it was. He made some cryptic remark about renovations.

I'm excited to see the resort. I've heard plenty of stories, mostly all hearsay, so seeing if those stories have any truth to them is exciting.

After getting changed, I exit the bathroom to see Zeke slipping on a yellow bracelet. I instantly bring attention to it since I'm pretty certain I know what the color means. I'm just not sure what it means to him or us.

I don't like to assume so I try to play it off. Zeke, however, calls me out and sets me straight. I need to stop with this self-doubt. It's only going to cause problems if I continue.

Walking to the resort was what I needed to clear my head. Zeke held my hand and pointed out things, seemingly just as excited to show them to me as I was seeing them.

When we approached the grand entrance, I was in awe. This place is stunning. It was like we stepped into another world. I tried not to gawk, but it was exactly like the stories I heard. Seeing it in person though, I was lost for words.

Zeke marched us straight to the front desk greeting the receptionist and asking for two red bracelets. I couldn't wipe the smile off my face.

As we are heading to what I'm assuming is the lounge, we are greeted by the most beautiful woman I've ever seen. She pulls Zeke into an embrace that catches me off guard. It seems a little too friendly.

"Hey there, handsome. We have it all set up for you. Oh, my lord. Would you just look at this beautiful specimen? You must be Gracie. I've heard so many things about you. Zeke said you were gorgeous, but his words do not give you justice at all. Those eyes, girl. I could get lost in those puppies." I smile at her exaggerated comments.

"She's mine. Plus look at the red bracelet. Gracie, this is the resort's General Manager, Rachel," Zeke says tucking me under his arm.

"I see you've switched to red too. Officially off the market, huh? You are one lucky girl, Gracie. It's nice to finally meet you," Rachel says, squeezing my hand.

I notice she has unusually large hands. That's when it hits me. "Oh...umm...nice to meet you too?" I say more like a question.

I'm not really sure how I should act. I feel stupid that I'm all of a sudden awkward. I look to Zeke for some guidance but end up getting it from Rachel.

"Oh, I see the light bulb just went off. Damn hands always seem to give me away. That and the Adam's Apple that I was blessed with. Believe me, I look much better like this than I ever did as a man. God at least provided me with dainty features in other regions," she says, pointing to her high cheekbones.

"I'm sorry and embarrassed that I don't know how to act. You are very beautiful, Rachel," I say.

"Don't be embarrassed or sorry, dear. It's a natural reaction really. You should have seen Zeke the first time we met. He was basically babbling," she responds laughing.

Zeke nods his head and laughs along with her making me relax. I think I'm more jealous of how smooth her skin is and how great she looks in that tailored pant suit.

Rachel leads me to a table in front of the stage as Zeke goes up and starts setting up. She tells me to order whatever I want, that it's on the house.

Before she leaves, she leans in and gives me a kiss on the cheek. "I said earlier that you were one lucky girl. He's the lucky one. You truly are a vision. Take care of him."

I'm a little confused. She looks like she is ready to cry. Surely, they didn't have a thing? I guess they may have? What is going on? This isn't the first cryptic or mixed message I've gotten since I got here.

A waitress comes to the table to take my order. I feel like I should drink wine or something classy, but I was never really good at picking out a wine I liked. So, I go for the beer I'm used to drinking. She quickly returns with my drink and a tray of crackers and assorted cheeses.

I jump in my chair when Zeke's voice comes over the microphone. I wasn't prepared for it to be that loud. He glances around the room as he introduces himself.

"For the new folks in the room, my name is Zeke Boyd, and I will be your entertainment for the evening. I see a few regulars have joined us as well, glad you could make it tonight. Welcome everyone," he says.

I sit in awe at listening to him sing. He's entertaining as well, getting the folks in the crowd involved in singing along. After his first set, he comes down and sits next to me making a motion to the waitress.

"Okay, I was going to let this be a surprise. The more I think about it, the more I think it may seem more like I'm blindsiding you," Zeke says, taking my hands into his.

I'm getting a little nervous now. He looks nervous and it's not helping things. I just sit here looking at him with so many questions flooding my head.

"I'm moving home," he says looking intently for my reaction.

My heart starts pounding in my chest and I almost let out a squeal. "That's why your condo is practically empty and Rachel looked like she was about to cry when she told me to take care of you," I say, putting all the pieces together.

"Not sure about Rachel, but you are correct on the condo part. My stuff is probably already in Maryland by now." He pauses and takes in a deep breath, "The moment I got home after the wedding I felt off. Hell, I didn't even want to leave and come back here in the first place. I already had conversations with my dad about it and got some sound advice. I've never once felt homesick in all the years I was gone. I felt it before I even left. I can do my job anywhere really, but I put in for a transfer and it was accepted. Between that and my parents' help, things just started falling into place. I'll be living at the apartment, much to Gram Pam's insistence. I also want to be a part of your life. I want us to be able to explore this relationship without the distance. If you will have me that is."

I have a lump in my throat and can barely get the words out. "You are amazing. I...I can't believe it."

"Believe it, sweet girl. Oh, and I got your return flight cancelled and refunded. William said to take your time coming back, he's got things covered."

"Wait, what?" I say, wiping a happy tear from my face.

"We are going back the way I came. I want to show you all the things I experienced when I drove here. It won't be three months long, though. Just a week. You game?"

I nod my head enthusiastically. I can't believe he did all this. I know it's not all for me, but it feels like I played a part.

He kisses my temple and says he has to get back up on stage. I pull out my phone and send of a text to Akia.

Me: Favorite status has been achieved.

Akia: He finally told you! I'm so happy for you!

Me: So you knew?

Akia: Babe, everyone knew but you. He begged us not to tell you.

I look from my phone to Zeke giving him a fake scowl and get a shoulder shrug in return.

# ZEKE

I got the reaction I had been praying for from Gracie. A look of utter joy came across her face and it made my heart smile. I was going to wait, but I kept thinking that blindsiding her was probably not the best way to go.

I'm about to sing the last song. The last song I may ever sing here. I feel a bit of sorrow but then think about what lies ahead.

I clear my throat, "I have a very special lady sitting in the audience. She took my breath away the first time I set eyes on her and she still does every time I look at her. I have some bad news, though. She's from Maryland and it looks like in order to keep my heart intact, I need to leave this wonderful city and go back home. I can remember the day I walked in here at eighteen like it was yesterday. This gig helped with spending money through college, and even after I was lucky enough to get a job in my field, I couldn't stop coming back to sing. This place has always been special to my family, and I'm honored that I was given the chance to make it special to me. Hopefully, this won't be my last song here ever. I'll be back to visit on vacation when I can. With that being said, this last song is dedicated to my sweet girl, Gracie."

I start the first part of *Sunday Morning*, by Parmalee as I see Gracie press her hands against her chest and smile. I see the glimmer of tears roll down her face as she listens closely to the words. I put my feelings into it trying to convey how much the words mean to me. There is truthfulness in the words and how they make me think of Gracie.

There's one line that goes, "Ain't nothing like the way you bring the crazy down." When I sing it, I look directly at her and she smiles. She knows that a simple touch of her hand has calmed me on a few occasions.

When I finish, I bow my head and send up a prayer of thanks for all God has given me. Cheers and applause fill the lounge and I'm humbled. The stage lights dim as I pack up my guitar.

Gracie comes up on stage and gives me a hug. "That song. Wow."

"I couldn't have written it better for you if I tried," I say, kissing her on the top of her head.

I say my goodbye's and try not to get emotional. This place has been a very important part of my life, of me growing up into a man. I've experienced some wonderful things here. A few kinky things as well.

Rachel is the last person waiting for me right by the exit. She's fanning her face wearing a wobbling smile.

"Hey, none of that. This is merely a see you later, never a goodbye. I'll be back on vacation, I promise," I say, pulling her into my arms.

"The only thing bad about being a woman...these pesky hormones," she laughs. "Right then, see you later, Zeke. Good luck in your new ventures. Keep in touch."

"I promise I will," I say, kissing her on the cheek.

I watch as she engulfs Gracie in a bear hug, kisses her cheek, and rushes off still fanning her face.

Once we exit, I stop and turn around taking a long look. Even though it makes me sad to leave, I feel a sense of closure on this chapter of my life. I ready to forge ahead and ready to get Gracie naked and into my bed.

I move the strap of the guitar case so it's at my back and swoop Gracie up into my arms. I take off running towards my condo. She lets out a squeal and we both start laughing.

I get to my front door and adjust her so I can pull my keys out of my pocket. I finally get the door open and walk through before setting her down on her feet.

I push the door closed with my foot and slip the guitar case off and to the floor. We are just standing there staring at each other, but I can see her chest rising with each quick breath.

We both take a step towards each other at the same time. My hands go into her hair as she grabs my shirt into her fists. Our lips meet slowly at first. I'm savoring her taste, the feel of lips, and the nibbles of her teeth.

There's a slow burn making its way straight to my cock. I start backing her down the hallway until I have the back of her legs against my bed. I can't hold back any longer as I take her mouth with more aggression. Her little sounds of pleasure have my heart racing. Taking off her sweater, I place a kiss on the side of her neck and down to her bare shoulders. I reach around and unzip the back of the dress as she moves the straps and the dress falls to the floor. Kissing the top of her ample breasts, I undo the clasp of her bra and watch in wonder as it also falls to the floor.

She quickly reached for my shirt, pulling it from my shorts and over my head. I tangle my hands in her hair and bring her lips back to mine. The softness of her breasts against my bare chest has my cock jumping and straining in my pants.

Gracie runs her hand down my chest and to my erection, cupping me through the material. I grind into her hand and throw my head back with a groan. Sitting on the bed, she releases the button and zipper slowly pulling both my shorts and my boxers down my legs until they meet her dress on the floor. I watch as she leans forward running the tip of her tongue over her lips. I pull her hair back so I can watch. The jolt of pleasure runs straight to my balls as she takes me into her hand, stroking me from base to tip.

"I've wanted to taste you for forever," she moans as she takes me into her mouth and looks up at me.

There's nothing sexier than having a beautiful woman look into your eyes as she sucks your cock. Having it be Gracie is even more incredible. Her eyes seem to bore straight to my soul.

"Fuck that feels incredible. If you keep it up, this will be finished before it gets started," I say, pulling her off me.

She lays back on the bed, fanning her hair out. "You look like an angel, so beautiful," I say looking over her bare torso.

I lift each leg and remove her boots tossing them to the other side of the room. Leaning over her, I kiss her belly and each hip as I glide her panties over her hips and down her legs.

She scoots herself up the bed, and I can't seem to stop staring. This amazing woman is finally in my bed. Not taking my eyes off her, I move to the nightstand and pull out some condoms.

"I'm on the pill and I'm clean," she says with such innocence.

"Works for me," I say tossing the condoms over my shoulder and climbing on the bed.

She lets out a giggle that stops as soon as run my hand over her breasts. Her nipples are hard and inviting, so I lean over and pull one into my mouth as my hand continues down. I can feel her heat before I even make it to between her legs. Her skin is so soft and smooth. My fingers start roaming down further until I can feel her wetness. She's already ready for me.

Rolling to my knees, I force them under her thighs, spreading her wide. Gracie starts pulling at her nipples grinding her ass into the bed. Fisting my erection, I guide myself to her opening, running it around her labia and over her clit.

"Look at me," I say as I press the tip barely inside.

Her eyes flutter open and meet mine. I lean forward placing my forearms on either side of her and run my hands up under her shoulder blades.

I grit my teeth as I slowly enter her. The sensation is almost overwhelming. Once fully seated, I grind my hips and watch as her mouth forms an O.

I feel her squeeze down on me and can no longer hold back from moving. I start moving in and out pulling down on her shoulders. I feel Gracie's ankles against my hip pulling me into her harder. She's meeting me thrust for thrust, and I start to feel the familiar tightening in my balls.

Reaching between us, I rub her hard clit until I can feel her start to pulse around me. Her whole body starts quivering, and I watch as her eyes roll. Her hands that were around my neck go flying up against the headboard as she let out an incredibly sexy moan.

Raising myself onto my hands, I use the leverage of her stiff arms to continue to pound into her with everything I've got. Beads of sweat are starting to roll down my forehead. With one last thrust, I slam my hands next to hers, emptying myself inside her with a growl. I grind my hips until the last pulse shoots through me.

We both are trying to catch our breaths as I glance down and see her looking up at me with a complete look of satisfaction.

"Fuck. That was...wow," I mutter out.

"Yeah, wow," she returns between breaths.

Rolling on my side, I pull her over into my arms. She entwines her legs with mine resting her face into my neck. Covering us up, I kiss her forehead.

"Worth every bit of the wait," I say, running my fingers over her back.

"Sure was, but promise we will never wait that long ever again," she breaths into my neck.

"Definitely a promise I won't have trouble keeping. I always keep my promises anyway," I laugh.

I feel her snuggle in deeper and let out a sigh. She's in my arms and in my bed and it's never felt more right. I listen as her breathing evens out as she falls asleep. I fall asleep soon after with a smile on my face.

## GRACIE

It's been a long time since I've woken up in bed with a man. Zeke is a human furnace and a bed hog. He's completely sprawled out on his stomach with his hands under his head and pillow. I have his elbow in my neck and his knee in my hip.

I wiggle myself out of the twisted blanket and laugh at how he doesn't move an inch. I take in the expanse of his back. His arms and chest are covered with tattoos, but he only has a single one in-between his shoulder blades with words.

I grab a long t-shirt from my bag and stand and watch him for a few minutes. I can feel myself getting turned on. The way he made my body catch fire last night was extraordinary. I don't think I've ever come that hard in my entire life.

I use the bathroom and wash my face, pulling my hair into a messy bun. Looking at myself in the mirror, I swear I'm glowing. I'm not sure if I should let him sleep or if I should wake him. I have no clue what he has planned, if anything.

I decide to move to the kitchen and look to see if there is coffee. I can't imagine him not leaving that unpacked since I saw him drinking a cup almost every morning I saw him.

His cabinets and drawers are almost completely empty. He has enough for two people but that's about it. I finally find the cabinet with the coffee and start the coffee machine, the only thing left on the counter. I knew he wouldn't have packed it.

I'm about to pour two cups when I feel arms go around me. I nearly jump out of my skin. It's going to take me a while to get used to his stealth ways. If I ever do.

"Smelled the coffee, thank you. You didn't have to, though. Why did you get up?"

"You practically pushed me out of bed. I see we are both not used to sleeping with someone. It's okay, though, I was awake."

"Sorry, we'll have to make sure we get a king size..." he says, trailing off.

I feel like he's holding back or catching himself from moving too fast, so I say, "California king is bigger."

He pulls me in tighter and reaches around to pick up one of the coffees. "California king it is then."

Zeke ends up cooking his famous omelet that we share. There's an easiness between us that I've never experienced before. It's like we are completely in sync.

"So, what's the plan? Catch me up with all that's going to be happening," I ask.

"Well, I had hoped to stay in bed all day, but that's my selfish side talking. We can basically leave whenever. If you don't mind helping me box up what little I have left, we can hit the road. I already have the condo up for sale and paid until the end of the year. My agent has a key, so I'm good there. I don't actually start my new job until after the New Year. I have the GPS in the truck already set for the trip back. I thought we would just play it by ear," he says, seeming to mentally check off things in his head.

"Well, I'm good with helping you. I'd had hoped to see a little of the city first, if that's okay," I say.

"Oh yeah, sorry. I didn't think about that. How about we take a trip to the Alamo? Can't leave without seeing that, and then tonight we can have dinner on the River Walk. Those are the hotspots. Then tomorrow, we can have a picnic at the lake that Bradley, Bruce, and Carrie got married. It's really nice there. Sound good?"

"Sounds great. In between, I can help you get packed and we can be on the road by Monday," I say, taking our dishes to the sink and washing them quickly.

"But first, shower sex?" he asks, lifting an eyebrow.

"Definitely shower sex, first," I laugh and take off down the hall with Zeke right on my heels.

## ZEKE

Shower sex is great. Shower sex with Gracie is perfection. Her body is incredible and just seems to mold with mine perfectly. The hard with the soft. She has this incredible ass and hips that I can dig my fingers into. Her breasts. No words. No matter where I grab, I get a handful of delectable goodness.

I've never known a woman to be so comfortable in her own skin. She doesn't primp or spend an ungodly amount of time on her appearance. She doesn't need to since she's beautiful just as she is.

Wearing a simple t-shirt dress and a pair of Keds, she looks like the all-American girl. Her hair piled up on her head, she grabs a pair of sunglasses and performs a little twirl.

"Gorgeous. You ready?" I say, slipping on a pair of loafers.

She nods her head walking towards the door. "I can't wait to see everything. Thank you for doing this for me."

"No need for thanks. Seeing that smile on your face is something I always want have a hand in."

I watch her smile the entire day. I've been here for ten years and never seen this place the way I'm seeing it through Gracie's eyes today. She bounces from historical signs to display cases and in and out of all the rooms. She practically floats through the courtyard and garden. I find myself bouncing right along with her. She makes me feel like a kid again exploring unknown places.

My favorite place in San Antonio is the River Walk. There is a buzz and wonder in the way there are lights in the trees all year long. You can hear the rustling of the water and the conversation of strangers. Yet, there is a peacefulness around you.

Gracie and I walk in and out of the different stores. I notice that she skips past the mainstream ones only focusing on the ones that are uncommon to the Maryland area.

She does, however, slip into the Harley store to buy herself a shirt with San Antonio on it. We end up settling into a little bistro that has an outdoor patio that overlooks the river.

"This is absolutely wonderful, Zeke. It's so beautiful. I can understand why you stayed. You kind of get pulled into it." She leans back and looks up. "But you can't see the stars. I would miss looking up and seeing all the stars."

"You are right. That's the first thing I noticed and remembered that first night home. I fell asleep that first night to the sound of crickets and a cool breeze blowing through the window. I realized then how much I missed it. Then a vision of beauty walked by the next morning and something clicked inside. It was like I was on this journey of finding solace. For the first time in my life, I felt like I knew where I finally belonged. Funny that is was where it had started. I was back home and I felt it. I felt like everything finally made sense."

"You know what? Let's get you packed up tonight and tomorrow and go ahead and head home. I had a really great day today, but I think I'm ready to get you home," she says, laying her hand on my arm.

"You sure? I don't want to feel like I'm cheating you out of seeing everything you want to see," I say, laying my hand on top of hers.

"I'm sure. I've never been off the East Coast, so I'm pretty excited to see more of the country, especially with you," she says, smiling and squeezing my arm.

# CHAPTER FOURTEEN

*Operation California King*

## ZEKE

It only took us a few hours to pack up the remainder of my things and get them in the truck. I have a hard truck bed cover that locks, so we got it all settled and locked up tight.

All that was left was my mattress that was now sitting on the floor, and a few towels. I'm not taking the mattress. It's old and my agent said she would get someone to take care of it for me. Our suitcases are in the truck as well except for what we need in the morning.

I strip down to my boxers and crawl into bed, flopping down onto my stomach spread eagle and let out a groan. I feel Gracie straddle my back and start massaging my neck and shoulders.

"Not used to manual labor I see. Hell that felt good to me. Got my blood flowing," she says, continuing to knead my muscles.

"I work out almost every day in order to keep this fine physique, my sweet girl, but damn, up and down those stairs just about killed me," I puff.

"You could have taken the elevator like me, you know?" Gracie laughs.

"Elevators are for wimps."

I get a pop to the top of my head. "You calling me a wimp?"

"If the name fits," I laugh, rubbing the spot she hit.

"Yeah, but who's sorry now," she says, popping me on the head again.

I quickly flip over, catching Gracie off guard, and knocking her off to her side. I reach over and pull her back so she's straddling me again.

She's wearing a tank top and sleep shorts that I remember her wearing back home.

"You have too many clothes on," I state.

"I do, huh?" she responds with a laugh.

"Yes, you do. I expect you naked and accessible when you are in my bed," I laugh, poking her in the side.

She pops up and in seconds has her tank top whipped off and her shorts and panties down around her ankles and kicked off to the side. She drops to her knees and I instantly cover my crotch.

"Easy girl, I plan on using this shortly," I say with a look of alarm on my face.

Laughing, she says, "I would never do anything to hurt the beast."

"Beast, huh? I like that you think so," I say, moving my hands and softly running my fingers down her chest and over her breasts. "Man, you have beautiful boobs."

"I'm glad you like them. Since they belong to you now," she says, settling herself on my thighs. Feeling her heat and wetness against my skin, I feel myself grow hard.

I slip my hands down and slip my boxers down exposing myself. "Well, the beast belongs to you now, sweet girl."

She takes me in her hand and lifts up, scooting forward. Leaning forward she places a hand on my chest and guides me to her opening. I place my hands on her thighs and squeeze as she slides herself down, taking me inside. The pleasure surrounds me. It seems to get better each time we connect.

She places both hands on my chest and starts to pick up speed, throwing her head back and making that sexy O face. I reach down between us to rub her clit and jack hammer up to meet her as she slams up and down on me.

Moving one hand off my chest, she leans back and I feel her reach back and caress my balls. She applies a little pressure to the underside, right above my ass, causing a surge of amazing ecstasy to the point I almost see stars.

"Fuck, Gracie, I'm going to come. Come with me, sweet girl," I almost yell.

"I'm there, Zeke, I'm there. Oh God," she moans, slamming down on me, grinding. I feel the familiar squeezing as I let loose inside of her. My toes actually curl, and I think I stop breathing.

Gracie flops down on me trying to catch her breath. I wrap my arms around her and stroke her hair and back.

"Whatever you did with you finger or fingers, I give full permission to do again," I say, kissing the side of her head.

She starts laughing and responds, "You don't want to know where I learned that from."

Her laughter causes her to squeeze me and I feel the evidence of the sex we just had flow between my legs.

"Oh my God, are you getting hard again?" she says, lifting up and releasing me from her.

"You were squeezing me when you laughed, I can't help it," I say. "What's got you laughing? You got me curious."

"You know I started out studying to be a vet, remember?" she says lifting up and giving me a look.

"Oh boy, forget I asked," I say, joining her in laughing.

She leans down and bites my chin continuing to laugh. "Yeah, you learn a little about anatomy that applies to both humans as it does animals."

"Okay, stop. That's just disturbing. I still give you permission to do it again, though," I say, taking her face into my hands and pulling her down to give her a kiss.

Gracie let out a yawn and slips to the side nestling into me.

"Good night, sweet girl. We start our journey home tomorrow," I whisper into her hair.

"I can't wait," she whispers back.

## GRACIE

I wake up again next to the Zeke furnace and half falling off the bed. I'm going to have to start fighting back for rights to my side of the bed.

We packed the coffee and coffee maker, so I get up and use the bathroom and go ahead and jump in the shower. I'm almost done when the curtain gets pulled back and Zeke jumps in, practically blocking the water.

"Zeke! I need to rinse the conditioner out of my hair," I say, tapping his shoulder.

"Sorry, just wanted to get wet quick," he says as he slips around me and turns me into the water stream. He runs his fingers through my hair, rinsing the conditioner out.

He grabs my conditioner bottle and puts a generous amount in his hands, running it over his head. He grabs his razor and proceeds to shave his head. I watch him in amazement of seeing how fast and precise he is at shaving, and I following behind his other hand to check the smoothness.

"I like using your conditioner. It's better than the stuff I usually use. Plus, I have your scent on me all day," he says finishing up.

"That's really neat to watch, you know. You are amazingly quick at that," I say, still watching him.

"I've been doing it for years. It's second nature now," he laughs.

"I'm going to step out and get dressed and let you finish up," I say, pulling back the curtain and step out wrapping in a towel.

"Did you sleep okay last night?" he says on the other side of the curtain, his voice echoing in the bathroom.

"Can you tell me how I can possibly regain my side of the bed when we sleep together?" I ask.

"Kick me? I don't know, babe. I don't realize I'm doing it," he says back.

"California King," I mutter.

"Yep, California King," he agrees.

## ZEKE

I feel bad that I'm apparently a bed hog. I've slept by myself for so long, it's just what I'm used to, I guess. I'm going to try to make a conscious effort to try not to do it on this trip.

We get the last of the stuff loaded in the truck and I'm starving, so I decide to make a stop at a little diner I liked to go to while living here.

"I'm going to do a little video blog of our trip. I wish I would have started it from the beginning, but I want to capture it now moving forward. Hope you don't mind being recorded?" she laughs, pointing her phone in my direction.

"This face was born to be on film, sweet girl," I joke, giving her my best side pose.

"Okay, entry day one on Zeke and Gracie's adventure. Operation, Home Bound. Wasn't there an old movie called that? Damn, I may need to change it," she says.

"Operation California King," I respond with a smirk.

"Perfect. Okay let me start over. Entry log day one of Operation California King. This is Zeke." I wave at her and then she changes the camera view from rear to front facing. "I'm Gracie and this is the start of what I know will be an amazing adventure. Right now, we are stopping at Zeke's favorite diner because his condo was empty and he's a muscle man that needs his nourishment and protein. Although, I am hungry, too. Because, well I like food. Anyway, this is our first stop. Many more to come." She leans over to me and lifts the camera so we are both in view. Kissing my jaw, she stops the video and jumps out of the truck.

I shake my head and laugh as I round the truck and throw my arm around her shoulder, "Muscle man, huh?"

"Well, yeah. Have you not seen yourself in the mirror? You have like zero body fat. Maybe I need to fatten you up a little on this trip. Nah, forget that, I like you just the way you are," she says, running her hand over my chest and stomach.

"I like you just the way you are too, sweet girl. We agree on that as far as not wanting to change anything," I say.

"Nope, you are perfect. Except for the bed hog thing," she says, laughing. "And hogging the water in the shower."

"You'll find more to complain about I'm sure. I'm not perfect, nobody is, but promise me you will tell me when I do something you don't like, please? I won't know if you don't tell me," I say, giving her a kiss.

"Same for you, too," she says, leaning into me.

"Nope, you are perfect as far as I'm concerned," I tease. "I'll tell you, I promise."

As we walk into the diner and are seated, Gracie says, "Thank you for this. For everything, really. I tend to joke about things a lot when I don't know how to express myself, but I really think what you are doing is incredible."

"This is just the beginning, sweet girl. Just the beginning."

## GRACIE

Breakfast is my favorite meal. I don't normally eat it in the morning, though. This diner is fantastic. It's like one of those old-time kind with all the chrome accents and waitresses in aprons. The food is incredible, too. I don't think Zeke even looked up but maybe once after his plate was set before him. I'm just as guilty. It's like I can't get enough. When we finish, we both lean back in the booth and let out a sigh, holding our bellies.

I take out my phone to capture the moment. "Hey everyone. I think we are both in a food coma right now." I flip to get Zeke in view and he has his head back and is rubbing his belly.

"I don't think I can move," he says, giving me a one-eyed glance and a smirk.

I flip the camera view back to me. "I'm not sure if we are going to make it out of here anytime soon. Thank God we are not on any kind of schedule," I laugh.

"I'm good, let's roll," Zeke says, scooting out of the booth and groaning.

I switch the camera view back so I can capture him. It takes him a good five minutes to finally get out of the booth, and I'm in tears laughing.

We make it out to the truck and Zeke opens my door for me. I think about how men don't seem to do this anymore and it makes me smile at how he still has old fashioned values instilled in him.

"First stop Dallas. I did a quick Google search and since we plan on just staying a day, I only want to see the JFK Memorial. It's not much more than structure, but I think it looks cool. Something to be captured at least," I say, switching the view back to Zeke who has already started down the road.

"What my girl wants, my girl gets," Zeke says, tapping the bill of his hat.

I'm doing sporadic videos of Zeke singing as we roll through town by town, and he suddenly makes a face. "Ummm, you may want to roll down a window," he says nervously.

"Oh my God Zeke. Is that from breakfast? Holy shit," I say trying to get the window down as fast as I can. I cover my face with my shirt and try not to gag.

"Okay, I need to sign off for now....I think Zeke needs to use the facilities," I laugh through my shirt.

"Babe, really? You need to record this?" Zeke laughs. "Okay peeps, I need to take a shit, so bye," Zeke says, grabbing the phone and stopping the record button.

"Seriously, when our kids see this, priceless," I say and stop realizing what I just said.

I glance over at Zeke and he's smiling from ear to ear. "I like that. You are thinking of us having kids? Sweet."

"If you keep expelling toxic gas, I won't be able to bear your children, so calm down there," I say, thinking that I slipped but he was all in. I don't know what to make of this whole situation.

"Zeke?" I ask hesitantly.

"Yeah babe?" he responds.

"I know this thing between us is all new and stuff. We are still getting to know one another, but can I ask what you are thinking it will lead to? What your thoughts are?" I ask.

"Oh, sweet girl. I'm all in here. I'm picturing you fat and pregnant in my bed and me doing everything in my being to make you happy. I've never felt a connection like I do with you. If you can handle my gas…why would I turn my back on that? I'm kidding, of course." He pulls the truck to the side of the road and turns to me.

"I'm going to be completely honest with you, because it's important to always be, but this thing between us…I feel it's the most real thing I've ever felt. The moment I met you I was struck dumb. I started planning our future. I knew you had reservations, and I want nothing more to squash them. I want you to see what I see," Zeke says.

"What do you see?" I ask, turning toward him.

"I see you and me and a house filled with love. Maybe a kid or two. But mostly I see a future with a beautiful woman that I see loving me...am I wrong?" he asks.

"No. You aren't wrong. I can see it, too. It may be too soon, but I need to say this...I love you," I say, looking him directly in the eyes.

"Wow, sweet girl. I love you, too, Gracie. I think I have since day one, if that's possible," Zeke says, reaching out and pulling me over to kiss me.

It's the softest and sweetest kiss. I could feel it throughout my entire body. With a press of his lips against my forehead, he groans.

"I don't want to ruin this moment, but if I don't get a restroom soon, this is going to end totally different that we both expect it to," he says, throwing the truck in drive and speeding down the road.

I can't help but to start laughing at the panic look on his face. I know I shouldn't because he really looks like he's uncomfortable. He whips his ball cap off and wipes his forehead with his forearm. There's sweat starting to roll down his face. I hear a loud rumbling coming from his stomach.

"There's a gas station right up there." I point down the road.

"Thank God," he mutters, speeding up.

He pulls quickly into a parking spot and jumps from the truck, breaking wind loudly.

I pull out the keys from the ignition and decide to go ahead and try to go to the bathroom myself. I sure in hell do not want to let one rip in front of him.

## ZEKE

We are about two hours into the drive, halfway to Dallas, when I fell a rumble roll through my gut. Gracie is recording me singing, and I can't stop myself.

I can't believe this is happening. I warn her to roll down the window and notice she's still recording. I grab her phone and stop the recording as she makes a statement about how priceless this would be to show our kids.

I see her eyes go large like she didn't mean to let that slip. I pull to the side of the road and tell her how I truly feel about her.

Hearing her say that she loves me is the most amazing feeling in the world. I may still be a little ahead of her in my feelings, but she's catching up.

Another rumble goes through my stomach and I know if I don't find a restroom quick, this moment will be ruined. Pulling into the gas station, I can't get out of the truck fast enough. I do a shuffle run to the bathroom.

Feeling a hundred times better and about ten pounds lighter, I pick up a few bottles of water and some snacks and pay. There's no sign of Gracie when I get back to the truck, but it's locked so I don't panic.

I feel arms slide around my waist and hands pat my belly. "Feel better?" Gracie says laughing.

"Much. Sorry about that," I respond, walking us towards the truck.

"It's natural. If it makes you feel any better, I feel a little lighter myself," she giggles.

We make it to Dallas, and Gracie is sleeping with her head against the window. I take a moment to just look at her. She looks so cute with her mouth slightly open and little bit of droll coming out of the side of her mouth.

I run my hand over her hair and she smacks her lips a few times, letting out a little snort.

Laughing, I softly say her name to try not to startle her. I watch as her eyes flutter open and she looks at me and smiles. Then a look of horror flashes over her face as she reaches up and wipes her mouth.

"First day on the road and we both embarrass ourselves. We make a hell of a pair," she says as a blush falls over her cheeks.

"Don't know what you are talking about. I wasn't embarrassed," I say, giving her a smirk. "Besides, you said it was natural. I'm sure we are going to learn a lot of somewhat embarrassing things about each other. I'll embrace each one of yours. Because that's what makes you unique and special."

I run my thumb over her bottom lip to the corner of her mouth. Lightly biting my thumb, she growls.

"How do you come up with just the right things to say?" she asks. "And turn me on with just a look?"

"Just speaking the truth, and that fucking growl...damn girl. Let's get checked in and get naked."

# CHAPTER FIFTEEN

*Backwards View*

## ZEKE

As we hit all the cities I stopped at all those years ago, it's like looking through a review mirror. This time I'm seeing it through Gracie's eyes. She has this enthusiasm about her that is contagious. Just like when we went through the Alamo, each place we visit is the best thing she's ever seen.

I can't believe how much I actually missed coming through the first time. Of course, I was eighteen then and had a different view on life and on things.

I mean, I was in Memphis for a week, and I don't think I got much further than Beale Street. Gracie was bouncing in her seat the whole drive to Graceland.

I felt it was a little too touristy and a bit tacky, but Gracie was in total amazement. When we were in the foyer, I whispered to her that I thought I saw the curtain move that hides your view from the second floor. She had a death grip on my arm the rest of the tour which had me laughing.

The house is smaller than I would have thought. I mean it was a mansion back in the day. Gram Pam's farm house is twice this size. The leopard lounge was so over the top, but Gracie was recording the whole time. Of course, I had to make the comment of wondering if anything would show up on the recordings later.

"Zeke, quit freaking me out. Seriously, I've got goose bumps now. Can we just skip the rest?" she says with a shiver.

"I'm sorry. I'll quit. I'm just teasing you, you know? I didn't mean to ruin anything for you," I say, regretting my actions.

She starts laughing and turns in my arms. "Karma is a bitch. Do you really think I'm that gullible? I wanted to come this week in hopes we could do some ghost tours in San Antonio. I love Halloween."

"Shit, I totally forgot about that," I say, kissing her forehead. "Let's do ghost tours in each city."

She starts bouncing up and down. "Yay! I'm so excited!"

From that moment on, we do research and do every ghost tour we can take part in. Her squeals make me laugh and at the same time, it pulls at my heart. To see her so happy is almost euphoric. Every moment makes me fall more in love with her, if that's even possible.

# GRACIE

I'm seeing and experiencing so much during this trip. Zeke is so attentive and makes sure that I'm getting to take part in everything I want. I feel like a queen.

I think I even have him trained to not be such a bed hog. Instead of kicking him, like he suggested, I curl into him or lay over him. He immediately turns and pulls me into him. It's a wonderful feeling, but the amount of heat he expels is something I'm still trying to get used to. Especially when I end up engulfed in his arms and legs.

I wouldn't trade it for anything.

When we make it to Nashville, Zeke informs me that he spent the majority of his time here. He then proceeds to tell me that he played with a band that is now a house hold name. They just got off their summer/ fall tour and were actually in town. He makes a few phone calls and the next thing I know we are heading to a private party.

To say I was star struck is a vast understatement. I was stiff and silent the majority of the time I was there. Zeke noticed something was off and pulled me to the side.

"Everything okay, sweet girl?" he asks.

"Ummm...I feel a little out of my element here and well...these are famous musicians. I'm not sure how to act," I say.

"They are just people like you and me. Hey, Lee. How about we play a song like old times?" Zeke shouts across the room.

I hear a hell yeah as Zeke pulls me with him to where the group is sitting. I stiffen again, but when I meet one of the wives, I'm put completely at ease.

I watch as Zeke sits within the group with his guitar, and suddenly, it's like I'm at a private concert.

I then realize that he could have been a part of this, all those years ago when he filled in for them, he could have stayed. He could be famous right now. His road lead him down a different path, and that road lead him straight to me. A road that is now leading him home. To the place I feel he belongs.

He beckons me over and I go and sit by his side. I can't help but join in with everyone else and sing along. I ask if I can record it and am giving a thumbs up by the lead singer. I'm going to hold these memories as one of the best of my life.

We get back to the hotel, and my cheeks hurt from smiling so much.

"That was amazing. I feel like I'm dreaming. I still can't believe that actually happened. I mean you know famous people, Zeke!" I spin around and bounce on my feet.

Zeke just shakes his head and smirks. "I guess I never really thought of it that way. I mean, I played with them ten years ago when they were just a bar band. If I didn't have a full time job, I could have gone on tour with them. They asked, you know."

"Holy shit. How cool would that have been? Seriously. How do you stay so nonchalant about it? I would be freaking out. The girls are going to die when they see this video. I can share it, right? I won't load it to my blog, but I have to share it with them," I say.

"Lee wouldn't have let you record it if he had an issue with you sharing it, babe. I'll text him to ask to be sure if you want, though," Zeke responds.

"Yeah, please do. I wouldn't feel right with putting it out there without approval. I'll send it to him to watch, if he wants to screen it or anything," I say, queuing up the video and sitting on the bed to watch it.

I'm bouncing on the bed and swaying back and forth as the video plays on my phone. I think the smile on my face gets even bigger. I realize that Zeke hasn't moved or has said anything, so I glance up to see what he is doing.

He's just standing there looking at me and smiling.

"What?" I ask, getting all self-conscious.

"You. Just you. I would be completely happy just watching you for the rest of my life. Addictive, just like the strongest drug. I can't seem to get enough of you. Don't ever lose that enthusiasm or zest for life. It's contagious, sweet girl. I can't believe how lucky I am," he says, walking over and lifting my chin to look up at him.

It never takes more than a touch and a look from him to send fire through my body. I blindly stop the video and set the phone down, never breaking eye contact.

Running my tongue over my top lip, I reach out and run the palm of my hands up the sides of his legs. I see his eyes darken and narrow just a bit as a rumbled growl rolls out from deep within his chest.

He takes both sides of my face into his hands and then runs the back of his fingers down the sides of my neck and over my shoulders. I feel like I could turn into a puddle.

I waste no time in getting his pants undone and over his hips, freeing him. I quickly glance down and take in the beautiful sight of his erection.

Using a fingertip to trace a vein, I follow with my eyes. I lean forward and use the tip of my tongue to follow the same path. Zeke stops his gentle movements and grips my shoulders. I think he's going to stop me but instead pulls me closer to him.

I slide my tongue around the tip and slowly take him into my mouth. I take him as far as I can, using a hand at the base so I don't gag. Taking his balls in my other hand, I gently roll them as I apply pressure to the area right behind him.

"That feels so good, sweet girl. Fuck, I love when you do that with your finger," Zeke says, rocking his hips forward.

We establish a rhythm and I apply a little more pressure, slipping the tip of my finger inside. As soon as I breach the tight rim, Zeke thrusts forward holding my head still. He lets out a loud "Fuck" and a moan, as I feel him release into my mouth. Looking up, I see his head thrown back and his face scrunched up as he continues to make short sporadic and jerky thrusts. The veins at his temples are throbbing, and it's the sexiest thing I've ever seen.

I release him and place my chin against his lower stomach and continue to look up at him. He releases a breath of air and runs his fingers through my hair.

Glancing down, he smiles, "I love you. I really loved that. Holy shit, sweet girl. You know how to make me lose all control. Now let me take care of you."

"I love you, too, and I'm good. I think I had an orgasm just watching you," I say, placing kisses around his abdomen and over a hip.

I feel him start to get hard again and let out a giggle. "You are a beast, aren't you?"

"Strip and crawl up the bed and I'll show you," he says, stepping out of his pants and pulling his t-shirt over his head.

I'm naked, flat on my back with his head between my legs within seconds. He has my body humming moments later and seeing stars soon after that.

❖❖❖

Our last stop before home was Pigeon Forge, Tennessee. This whole trip has been an experience I will never forget. I've recorded so many amazing videos. I got approval to share the impromptu jam session, but I didn't want to load it to anywhere too public. I like my privacy and I'm sure those guys do as well. So, I decided to make a special album on Facebook. I have my privacy settings pretty tight on there.

I was still pretty surprised. My video was shared by almost all of my two hundred friends and it seemed to go viral from there. My notifications started blowing up. My friend requests blew up. I got a whole lot of positive comments and some that were outright negative. The most surprising thing was the amount of private messages Zeke started receiving with women's phone numbers and comments about how they were more woman than I'd ever be.

At first, he would respond with comments of how shallow people didn't deserve his attention. He ended up just handing me his phone and asking me to delete and block them.

I spent most of the trip from Nashville to Pigeon Forge on both of our phones. I don't get the nerve of people, and I regret not making the videos not sharable. Over the years, it's become easier to remove tags and make posts less accessible. All you have to do is edit the original post and all posts that were shared then become hidden or changed to the way you want them.

It took me a while to figure it out, but by the time we got to our hotel, the notifications and messages stopped. A seed was planted in my head, though, of self-doubt. It's a battle and something I struggle with constantly. It's not justified and I'm confident for the most part, but the comments that I did read made me get in my head.

I use the bathroom and take a quick shower. I can't seem to make eye contact with Zeke. I find an outlet and plug in my almost dead phone from all the activity today, and just crawl into bed. I close my eyes and mentally chastise myself for giving into my insecurities.

I feel Zeke crawl into bed and pull me against his naked body. My body instantly reacts and I try to shut it down.

"What's going on in that head of yours, sweet girl? You've gone into a different world," he says, kissing my neck.

"It's nothing...I'm being stupid," I huff.

"It's not stupid if it makes you hurt. I can almost feel your pain. Talk to me," he says, rolling me over and taking my chin and forcing me to meet his eyes.

"Some of the comments were just cruel. I know it shouldn't bother me, but they still hurt. I have no reason to doubt this, what we have. Your actions speak louder than your words. I see your love when you simply look at me. I know this. Then the little insecurities rear their ugly head and I just...let it get to me. I shouldn't care what other people think, and I don't...or at least I keep telling myself I don't," I say, breaking eye contact as a tear breaks through and rolls down my cheek.

"You are mine. I'm proud and lucky that you are mine. I thank God every day that an incredibly beautiful woman even gives me the time of day, yet alone share these same feelings of love. I get where you are coming from. I won't tell you to simply not listen to what people say, that's easier said than done. I know this. I can only continue to show you through my actions and my words. Please know this...I love you, body and soul and everything else I can think of. I can't imagine my life without you in it. When I think about my future, you are there, every step of the way," Zeke says, laying a gentle kiss to my lips and wiping the tears that start flowing.

"I love you, too. There is no doubt of my feelings for you. I see you when I dream of my future. I hate that I have these moments of doubt, I really do." I take a cleansing breath. "You make me feel special. I hope I never get used to it. I don't think I will. You have this ability to always say just the right things and with sincerity that I will never question," I say, rolling on top of him.

I grind myself against his hardness and the feeling of flesh on flesh ignites a fire deep in my core. With a quick reach between us, I draw him to my opening and practically impale myself on him. Fully seated inside, I grind my hips as he grabs me by the waist and thrusts up.

We practically chant "I love you" as we meet thrust for thrust until both of us reach our peak, and I fall on top of him completely spent.

I don't remember falling asleep, but I must have fairly quickly. I wake to a knock at the door.

## ZEKE

I don't get her insecurities fully, yet I do. The standard that society places on woman are unrealistic. You either have to be paper thin or have surgical implants that make you look truly unnatural.

Gracie doesn't need to be anything but her. She's incredibly beautiful. She has full breasts that feel heavy in my hands. I can dig my fingers into her hips and ass, and I can't imagine how I was ever attracted to anything less. The dimples at the bottom of her spine at the top of her ass are nothing less than kissable.

I can't even begin to tell you how it makes me feel when I feel her grip me from inside and have her lose all control. Her whole body just shakes and convulses when she comes. It makes me feel powerful that I'm able to please her in this way.

I want to go all Tarzan and pound on my chest.

I can tell that she starts breaking down and getting into her head through our drive. I can only image the comments she was subjected to, I saw a few and from the messages I started getting, I was feeling frustrated myself. I'm so glad she figured out how to shut that shit down. She's pretty savvy with technology. I was going to do my thing once we got to the hotel, but she figured it out.

While she was in the shower, I called and ordered our breakfast for in the morning. I want to try to continue to make this memorable for her. This is a setback, but I hope it just make our bond stronger. I poured my heart out to her. I only hope she realizes that I wouldn't be the same without her.

I'm woken up by a knock at the door and slip on my boxers to answer it. The smell from the tray of food has my stomach growling. A few seconds later, there is another knock and I'm greeted by a delivery of flowers. Yeah, I know. I got this.

I see Gracie stir and roll to her back, she quickly sits up against the headboard as the cover rolls over her and falls to her waist. She tries to cover herself, but I shake my head and she lets them fall back down.

I move to the bed and place the tray in her lap. Kissing the top of her exposed breasts and then I lean down and kiss the pouch of her stomach.

She raises the lid off of one of the plates and lets out a sigh. "Although I don't want this to end, I need to get back to work in order to get rid of all this extra weight I've gained on this trip."

"You've uncovered my evil plan. Plump you up so I have more to grab hold of," I say, raising a piece of bacon to her lips.

Laughing, she takes a huge bite, almost nipping my fingertips in the process.

I can't stop staring at her breasts. I love how comfortable she seems after our conversation last night. She notices the flowers on the bedside table and mentions how incredible I am.

Again, I know this. I just need to make sure she never forgets it or how incredible she is to me.

The weather is seasonably warm, hovering around the mid-seventies. The trees have changed and are vibrate orange and red in color. The smoky mountains are simply gorgeous this time of year.

We spend the day at Dollywood. It's their harvest festival, and it's incredible watching some artists carve pumpkins. Gracie squeezes my hand as she points out her favorites and captures it on video.

We act like teenagers hoping from ride to ride and I'm pleased that she loves the roller coasters just as much as I do. We are both exhausted by the end of the evening and simply strip and crash in bed.

The next morning, we pack up our things and start the journey home. I'm excited to get into a routine, even though I won't start my new job until after the New Year. I have things I intend on doing to put down some real roots. I've heard you will know if it is meant to be or not by vacationing with someone. I think Gracie and I are it. This journey home has been nothing but amazing, and I'm thankful that I got to experience it with her. It was closing chapter in my life and beginning a new one that I believe will be filled with many new adventures.

# CHAPTER SIXTEEN

*Roots*

## ZEKE

I want really want to stall and draw out what's left of this trip. We haven't discussed what's going to happen once we return home. I see the sign for our exit and start tapping the steering wheel nervously.

"Mind if we make a stop?" I ask.

Gracie is staring out the window and I know she's in her head. "Gracie," I say again, looking back and forth from the road to her.

"Sorry, what did you say?" she asks, looking at me and giving me a sad smile.

"I wanted to know if you minded us making a stop. Even though it's legal, I feel like I committed a crime transporting weed across state lines," I laugh.

"Oh, sure. That's fine," she says, shrugging and turning to look back out her window.

"Hey...look at me," I say and wait for her to look back. "This trip is almost over, but that's all that's over, right? Why so sad?"

"I'm just not ready to get back to reality. I wish it wasn't over," she says, trying to smile.

"Remember, I'm still on vacation, but I planned on helping you around the farm. We are going to see each other every day," I say.

"I'm going to miss my human furnace and bed hog," she whispers.

"You can just stay at the apartment with me. Problems solved and no missing anything," I respond, trying to gauge her reaction.

"You want me to move in with you?" she says with a bit of excitement returning to her voice.

"I guess I just thought that would be the next step. If you feel it's too soon, we can do a couple nights here and there. Better than going cold turkey. I've had you beside me every night for the past week. I'm not sure I can go back to sleeping alone," I say.

"I want to talk to Pam first. I need to make sure she'll be okay," Gracie says.

"I need to talk to Gram Pam as well. If she's not busy, let that be the first item on our agenda. But first, let me make that old man Sun happy and get this weed out of the truck," I say, reaching out and grabbing her hand.

All we get is a "Bout time" from Sun as he grabs the baggie and shuffles his way to a back room.

Flower gives us each a kiss on the cheek and shuffles her way back following him. Gracie and I are left standing in their entrance way and all we can do is laugh. I really hope I'm as cool as they are when I get to their age. Hell, I just pray I make it that far.

## GRACIE

Pulling up the drive, I'm exhausted, but I want to talk to Pam. I feel like I need to get her blessing. We've become very close, and I look up to her like she's my real grandmother.

Zeke doesn't take any of the bags out of the truck. I'm sort of glad because I really want to take them into the apartment and not the house. Pam is sitting in the living room watching TV when we walk in.

She goes to stand but Zeke tells her not to and pulls me over to sit on the couch with her.

"Well you two look serious. How was the trip? I watched all those videos you took, looked like you had a really good time," Pam says.

Zeke takes the lead, which I'm grateful. "Well two things. But to answer your question, we had a wonderful time. Didn't we?" he says to me. I nod and smile and he continues. "We are in love and I want Gracie over at the apartment with me, and I want to buy some of your land to build a house."

The second part catches me off guard but has me smiling knowing he's serious about staying. I know his is but nothing is more reassuring than investing in land and a house.

"Well that was straight and to the point. But...I sort of had something else in mind. I could tell from the videos that you two had become really close, and I had a feeling something like this would happen. So, I started thinking, actually I set things in motion the moment I knew you were coming back home..." she hesitates and has us both motioning for her to continue.

"This house is getting too big for me. I'd rather have the apartment, but Lord knows I wouldn't be able to handle those steps all the time. So, I talked with Bruce about adding on. He started actually pretty quickly. I'm going to have my own little quarters right off the mud room. I'll have my own entrance, but will still be able to access the house if I need. Or if I need help, you will be able to get to me quicker," she says stopping.

"That sounds like a really good plan, but what does this have to do with me buying land and building a house?" Zeke asks.

"Let me repeat, if I need help, you will be able to get to me quicker," she says smiling.

Zeke and I look at each other puzzled. "I still don't get what you are trying to say here," I say, squeezing her hand.

"Oh, you are no fun. I thought you were smarter than this," she says laughing. "I want you two to have the main house. Granted it needs a little updating and remodeling, but it's yours to do whatever you want. Make it your own."

"Are you serious?" I ask, getting a little excited. "I love this house. I can't believe you would do that, what about your other grandkids or family? Zeke and I aren't even blood."

"I never want to hear that kind of talk from you. You are just as much my family as anyone else. I talked to them all about it and they all agreed it should be yours. Akia was the only other choice, and her and Doug already have started building. But I wanted you to have it, anyway."

"Gracie, I know how much you love this house and the farm, and Zeke, I remember how you seemed to love it when you worked here. I'm just glad you finally got your head out of your ass and realized this is and will always be home."

"I'm touched and would be honored to call this my home. As far as updates and remodeling go, this house doesn't need much. A big screen over the mantel, converting your downstairs bedroom into an office. Oh, and we don't need five bedrooms upstairs. I plan on Gracie spitting out a few of my kids, but I think we can give up the small one next to the master to convert into an attached bathroom and walk in closet..." Zeke says, standing and looking around with a huge smile on his face.

"Woah, slow down there, cowboy. Two kids max, and I thought I rambled. Do I have a say in anything of this?" I ask, getting to my feet.

"Of course, you do, I'm just throwing out ideas. What you got?" he asks.

"Nothing...I got nothing to add. It sounds perfect," I say, smiling and walking into his arms. "I especially like the idea of a huge closet."

"Sound like an old married couple already," I hear Pam mumble and laugh. "I'm heading to my room for the night. I love you two. Good night."

She pulls Zeke's head down and kisses the top of his head and gives me a kiss on the cheek, disappearing into her room.

"Wow. I'm a little overwhelmed. Did that just happen?" I ask, burying my face in Zeke's neck.

"I think so. Damn, not even home five minutes and we have a house. Seems to me that our destiny is happening without our intervention. Pretty amazing actually. I knew the moment I saw you things were going to be good," he says, kissing my temple.

"So, what now? I'm not sure what to do or where to go," I laugh.

"Well depending on when the addition is done and when we can get started on the upstairs, I say we stay at the apartment. We never did really get an answer on that, but I don't want to disturb Gram Pam," he responds.

"Can we just stay here tonight? No funny business though. I don't know if there's anything over there yet and I'm beat," I say, backing up to look into his eyes.

"Yeah, true. I'm tired, too. Let me go out and get a few bags so at least I'll have clothes in the morning," he says, smacking my ass and walking to the door.

"I'm going to head up and get ready for bed," I say to his back.

He throws his thumb up in the air, making me laugh. I stand and take a look around imagining some little changes I can make. I have a house. I have a house and I have Zeke. I smile all the way up the steps picturing framed photos of us and our family lining the walls. I glance into the master bedroom and think about what color I'm going to paint it and how that California king is going to look sweet in there. I'm in bed and half asleep when I feel Zeke crawl under the covers and pull me against him in a spooning position.

I fall asleep with his heat warming my back and dream about all the things I've always wanted to do in this house and now can do them with the added bonus of a man at my side.

## ZEKE

I wake up the next morning to an empty bed. I hear noises coming from downstairs and the smell of food and coffee hit my nose. My stomach growls, and I instantly jump up and throw on my sleep pants and a t-shirt. I quickly use the bathroom and wash my face and hands. I went a few days without shaving so I can see the dark hair start to show on the top of my head. My beard needs trimmed as well. I look a little ragged. Shrugging my shoulder, I rush down the steps to find Gracie and Gram Pam standing side by side at the stove laughing.

"My two favorite girls," I announce and both of them jump. Laughing, I walk over to the coffee pot and pour myself a cup.

"You had to hear me coming down the steps, why so jumpy?" I say, taking a slow sip and looking at them over the rim.

"For as muscular as you are, you have light feet. I've told you that you are ninja like all the time, Zeke," Gracie says, coming over and giving me a kiss. She scratches my beard and points over to the table. "Sit, breakfast is almost finished."

After breakfast, I throw on some work clothes. I walk outside and see Uncle Bruce coming around the side of the house.

"Hey, see you made it home. Did Mom tell you yet?" Uncle Bruce asks, giving me a big hug.

"Yeah, and I'm still a little shocked. I was planning on helping Gracie out around the farm, but I sort of want to help you, if that's alright?" I ask.

"Absolutely. The faster we get this done, the faster we can start getting things done in the main house for you and Gracie. Have you thought about what you want to do, if anything?" he asks.

I run through some of the plans that I expressed last night and a few more I thought of this morning. "I would like to turn the downstairs bedroom into an office. There are going to be times I can bring things home instead of working late at the precinct. Plus, there's opportunities for some consulting work in D.C. I really don't want to have to go down there if I don't have to, so it will give me somewhere to work. But I'm also thinking of putting in a half bathroom as well, if that will work," I say.

"That room is fairly large, I don't think there will be an issue with breaking it into two rooms. You don't need much for a half bath either. Sounds like a great plan," Uncle Bruce says.

We walk to the side of the house and I'm stunned. "You did all this in a week?" I ask.

"Hell no. We've been working on this since we found out you were coming home and Mom got a bur up her butt to give you the house, which we all think is fantastic, by the way. I'm good, but I'm not that good," he says laughing.

Gracie comes bouncing out of the house with her jeans and work boots and a flannel on. "Hey, Bruce. Your son is a damn slave driver. I called to see when he wanted me back in rotation and he said to get my lazy ass to the barn, lovingly of course." She stops short and looks at the addition that looks done from the outside. "Oh my God. I guess I am gullible after all. You told me this was going to be an extra storage shed for the ATV's in order to make room in the garage. I can't believe I fell for it."

"I was wondering how the hell you didn't know what was going on. From the outside, it looks just about done," I say, pulling Gracie into my arms.

"We need to bust through to the mud room, which Mom wanted to be last to keep the surprise, and finish up some painting. We can start moving her things over in a couple of days," Bruce says, opening the outside door and motioning us in.

"Holy shit. This is amazing," I say, pulling Gracie inside with me.

There's a full open floor plan with high vaulted ceilings. The one side is completely made up of floor to ceiling windows and French doors. Bruce explains that eventually he's going to build her a deck so she has a place to sit outside. I see the section that is partially framed in, ready to be busted through to the mud room. It's beside the kitchen which has all the top of the line appliances.

"This is really gorgeous, Bruce. Okay, I need to get going before William starts blowing up my phone," she says as she gives me a kiss and Bruce a hug and bounces out of the door.

"That girl has never bounced. Stomped, yes, but never bounced," Uncle Bruce says smiling.

"Really? Well I remember her pony tail always bouncing or swinging. Anyway, she seems to bounce all the time around me," I say, pulling the bill of my hat down and smiling.

"Okay enough about Gracie, what do you need me to do?" I ask, clapping my hands and rubbing them together.

I end up finishing up the last of the painting. I'm surprised that there is no smell. Bruce is moving in a new sectional that he bought for his mom as Gram Pam stands pointing to where she wants it set up. There's a few of his guys finishing up the door after they broke through the wall.

Bruce has one of the largest construction companies in the area. It works in his favor when he needs stuff done for the family. His vision is incredible and his talent is top notch. What he has built for his mom is really gorgeous. It's new and updated, yet fits into the whole farm house extension. It blends in perfectly and seamlessly.

The front door suddenly opens and I see Uncle Bradley and Aunt Carrie walk in with their arms full of groceries. My mom and dad come in shortly after carrying bag as well. My mom looks up and sees me and drops the bags. My mom is tiny. I mean really tiny. But she is fierce. She pushes everyone out of her way and practically tackles me.

"My baby boy is home! You are really home!" She grabs my face and starts kissing me all over.

"Mom, come on. You are practically slobbering on me," I say laughing.

"But my baby is home," she says, squeezing the life out of me.

"Did someone order pizza?" I hear Gracie's voice call out as she comes in carrying a few boxes of pizza. "They were banging on the main house door. Someone owes me five bucks I paid for the tip."

Bradley digs out his wallet and pulls out five bucks. "She's cute, Zeke, but a cheap ass."

"She's beautiful and that ass is definitely not cheap. It's luscious, actually," I say, stepping up and taking her ass into my hands.

"I was just teasing, guys! Stop getting all alpha male, Z-man," Uncle Bradley says laughing.

We end up standing around the long island that separates the kitchen from the living room eating pizza, talking, and laughing. I look around and think about all the times that I spent alone eating pizza in my condo. I realize that on any given night, at any given moment, I could have had this with my family, enjoying a simple night of pizza, together. But since I felt the need to explore the world and leave them all behind, I missed out on it all. A great evening with my family and the girl who fits into the fold perfectly. I vow to always remember this moment and never forget how it made me feel. It's like I'm feeling this sense of comfort, a feeling of solace that I've never known to exist. I'm finally where I need to be and it's never felt more like home. The place where I truly belong.

# CHAPTER SEVENTEEN
*Beginnings*

## GRACIE

We got Pam all moved in and settled. It seems that she's really enjoying her new space because she has been scarce in the main house. The renovations are coming along quick. Zeke's office and the powder room is done. The master bathroom is almost done, too. We ordered a new bed, a California Kind of course, which should be in next week. Bruce even went ahead and build his mom a deck outside her French doors.

I miss her, though. I spent many mornings cooking breakfast before I made my daily rounds with her. It's almost Thanksgiving and it's a rough time of year for me. I lost my mom a few years ago to cancer right after Thanksgiving. I tried to convince my dad to let me move back home, but he insisted that I needed to live my own life and that he was fine. I still worry about him.

I'm feeling a little depressed, which happens around this time, of course. Pam was always there to help talk me through it. She means so much to me and I get emotional just thinking about it.

It's stupid because she's literally steps away, but her constant presence just isn't there anymore.

Zeke is still sleeping since I seem to wake before the sun even starts to peak over the horizon. I make a pot of coffee and pour myself a cup. I've been feeling really emotional lately and think it's probably just due to being around that time of the month. I wrap myself into my favorite quilt and step outside. The air is crisp and there is no sound to be heard.

I hear a clearing of a throat and realize it must be Pam on her deck. Excited, I round the corner of the addition and see her sipping on her own cup of coffee and wrapped in a blanket.

"Hey, you," I say, stepping on the deck and taking a seat next to her.

"Hey, Gracie. It's a beautiful morning, huh?" Pam says, reaching out and grabs my hand.

I instantly start crying. I don't know why but I can't seem to stop. I get this overwhelming feeling of total sadness.

"Oh honey, why are you crying?" she says, squeezing my hand.

"I have no idea," I say, laughing and crying at the same time. "I miss you? It's that time of the month? It's that time of the year? I don't know."

"Oh, sweetheart. I know I haven't been that present, but I really love this place. I want you and Zeke to have your privacy, too. I don't want you to think that I've abandoned you. I'm only a few steps and a little door away from you," she says, reaching out and wiping the tears from my face. "I know this is a hard time of year for you. Is your dad going to come to Thanksgiving this year?"

I take a deep breath and blow it out. "I think so, I hope so. He looked good the last time I saw him and sounded good. He said that he's going out and hanging with some of his old buddies again."

"That's good. I know it's hard. Everything okay with you and Zeke?" she asks.

"He's perfect, Pam. I don't know what I did to deserve a man like him. He's loving and attentive and funny. I really love him. I've never felt this way about someone before in my life. It's almost unbelievable." I finally stop crying.

"Gracie. You deserve happy. I'm happy for you and for Zeke. Never doubt that you should have this happy. You both deserve it," she says.

"Will you come make breakfast with me like old times? I really think I need that right now. We can talk about our plan for Thanksgiving. I still want everyone to come here like all the other years. I hope no one thinks that will change with all that has happened lately. This is still your house and I want to keep on with the tradition. We can open the door to your place and fill both places with everyone," I say, getting excited.

"That sounds like a wonderful idea. Help me up and let's cook and plan," she says laughing.

Just having Pam back in the kitchen helps settle me. When Zeke finally comes down, he kisses us both and mentioned how much he missed us cooking breakfast. Even not being around it much, he gets it. He felt that connection of having Pam around. I know I need to let it go and let her live her life just as I need to live my own, but it's just not that easy.

## ZEKE

I wake to the smell of food and voices from downstairs. I slip on a pair of sleep pants and make my way to the kitchen. I know that I haven't been here through the years, but I know how much Gracie has been missing Pam. She has seemed depressed lately or off, I'm not sure. Seeing them together in the kitchen brings a sense of happiness. The smile on my girl's face is breath taking and I want to make sure I keep it there.

We finish up breakfast and I tell Gracie that I'll clean up and to go ahead and head out to make her rounds. I gather all the dishes from the table and head over to the sink.

"You know about her mom, right?" Gram Pam asks.

"Yeah, she lost her around this time, right? Is that why she's been so emotional lately? I know she misses you, too, but it seemed like it was more. I've been trying to be there, but she doesn't seem to want to talk about it and I've not tried to push the issue. I don't want her to be sad. I've felt lost trying to make her happy or try to make it better."

"Zeke, just keep doing what you are doing. She loves you. I wasn't thinking myself, and I'm sorry I didn't realize how my lack of presence would affect her so much," Gram says. "She's been a part of the family for a few years now. I felt like I needed to step back and let you to have your privacy."

"I love that she's so welcomed into this family because I plan to make it official. I feel like she's more a part of it than me. I'm here now and I plan to step up and change that," I say, giving her a hug.

"Ezekiel James, you need to stop that. You are a part of this family. You were lost for a while, but you are back now. We are grateful to have you and I personally look forward to many years of memories."

"Many, many years. You better be prepared to live into your hundreds, because I need to make up for lost time," I say, holding her tighter and kissing the top of her head.

## GRACIE

I feel better after being able to cook with Pam this morning. These damn emotions have just been overwhelming. I feel like I could cry at the drop of a hat. I know that it's about that time of the month, but it seems like more. I feel exhausted all the time and I'm constantly horny. It's like I could just jump Zeke's bones every time he is around.

I'm oiling up the saddles and putting them up when I get a sharp pain. It makes me bend over and grab my stomach. I take a few breaths and the pain subsides. *What the hell was that?*

Zeke is hanging with his dad tonight, so I called Akia to hang out. I finish showering and look at my pills and notice that I'm on the week I should start my period. I have yet to start. I shrug it off and throw on a pair of jeans and a hoodie and head out to meet up with Akia.

I get to the restaurant the same time Akia does. We walk in together arm and arm and get seated.

"I have some news that I don't want you to share just yet. It's early, but I need to tell someone...I'm pregnant," she says, smiling from ear to ear.

"Oh my God! That is wonderful! How far along are you?" I ask.

"Almost three months. I think it happened on the honeymoon. We wanted to try right away, but I never thought it would happen so fast. My body has taken on a mind of its own. I mean, my boobs have swelled and I seem to tingle. It's the weirdest thing ever, but so far, no sickness. I can tell something is different, but I feel normal at the same time. It's really weird," Akia laughs, placing a hand on her belly.

"I'm so excited for you! That is amazing. I know how much you wanted to start a family right away. What's Doug feeling?" I ask.

"He wants to yell it from the rooftops. It's killing him not to start handing out cigars. He's been extra attentive, if that is even possible. I mean the guy is normally all in to taking care of me. Now? I'm surprised he doesn't want to wipe my ass when I take a shit. He probably does, but I need to draw the line there," she laughs.

"Oh Akia, I'm so excited for you," I say, reaching out to grab her hand.

"You know you will be the Godmother, right? Gracie, you are my best friend and I've always thought of you as a sister. I want you to be a part of my little baby's life. You know the only reason you weren't my maid of honor was because I wanted you paired up with Zee. Plus, Macy would have had a breakdown if I didn't ask her. I had no problem giving her that responsibility. There's no way I will let her have responsibility of my child. So, will you?" she asks.

At this moment, I'm overcome with emotions and start crying uncontrollably. "Of...course..." I choke out.

"Oh my God. Why are you crying? It's not that big of a deal, babe," Akia says, coming around the table and hugging me from behind.

"It is a big deal, Akia. God, I'm so honored," I say, wiping my face. "Don't mind me. It's that time of the month. I've been full of emotions lately. I broke down this morning with Pam. That and with it being this time of year, I'm just an emotional mess. I'm okay...please people are starting to stare," I say, rubbing her arm that is around me trying to laugh it off.

"Wait till you get pregnant. Girl, I'm crying because you are crying and you know I don't cry easily," Akia says, taking her seat and wiping the tears from her face. "Doug keeps thinking he's doing something wrong when I break down out of nowhere."

"Look at us," I say laughing. "You would think I was pregnant too," I say and then stop laughing. "I'm on the pill. I take it the same time religiously every day. I can't possibly be pregnant."

Akia throws up her hand and yells, "Check. Girl, you know Zeke has super powers, right? The pill's disclaimer isn't a one hundred percent guarantee for a reason. I'm so excited. We could be fat and pregnant together. I'll have a girl and you'll have a boy. They'll grow up and get married and give us grandbabies."

"You are getting way ahead of yourself," I say nervously. "I'm not pregnant."

"Just give me this, will you? Come on. We can grab some ice cream and pregnancy tests and watch girly movies. Regardless of the results, this will be fun." She boxes up the remainder of the food and pays the check. "Don't look at me that way. I'm not letting this food go to waste. Momma and baby need nourishment. Which you will need, too."

"Akia. Stop. I'm not pregnant for Christ's sake," I say. I can't stop laughing at her excited actions. This is so not like her. "Okay, if it will make you happy, let's go. Just don't be disappointed when the results are negative."

◆◆◆

Five pregnancy tests line the bathroom counter. All are positive. Akia is bouncing up and down, while I'm pacing the bedroom in disbelief.

"How?" I say.

"Well, when two people love each other, the daddy sticks his penis in mommy…" Akia starts and I begin laughing and crying at the same time.

"Stop! Smart ass. You know what I mean," I say, plopping down on the bed and cradling my head in my hands.

"I'm sorry, but I couldn't help it. Are you okay? I mean you are happy about this right? Here I am making fun and you could not want this. You want this right?" Akia says, sitting beside me and rubbing my back.

"I don't know what I think right now. I need to process this. I mean, yeah, I guess I'm happy. I don't know if I'm ready for a baby, though. I mean, Zeke and I are still getting to know one another. It's just happening so fast. What if he thinks I planned this to trap him or something?" I say, trying to get my head around this situation.

"Really? You think Zeke isn't going to pound his chest like Tarzan and be excited about this? You know Zeke better than any of us. The grown-up Zeke that is. All the time you spent trekking across the country home together you get to know someone really fast that way. Besides, the odds of you getting pregnant on the pill are astronomically low. This is meant to be. I just know it," Akia says, standing and pulling me up to my feet. "So now our pregnant asses can indulge in guilt free ice cream together. Come on, I'm in the mood for a Rom Com."

I place my hand on my belly and smile. I'm pregnant. I can't believe it. Akia is right. Zeke is going to be ecstatic. We grab a container of ice cream each and queue up a movie. We both end up falling asleep and are woken by Zeke's arrival home.

Akia stretches and gives us both a hug and a kiss and heads home. I'm nervous. I'm not sure if I should tell him right now or what to do.

I clean up the ice cream containers and turn off the TV. Zeke has already headed up to bed.

"Babe, what the fuck is this?" I hear him yell from upstairs.

Shit. I left the tests out on the counter. Is he mad?

# ZEKE

I haven't had a whole lot of time to spend some one on one with Dad. It seems like we all get together in groups, which is amazing, but I've been wanting it to be just him and me.

"Did you really know Mom was the one the first time you met?" I ask as we sit down to eat at a local restaurant.

"Absolutely. Your mom did, too, it just took a while to break through the wall of insecurities she had. Your mom can be one stubborn woman. You get that from her, you know?" he says chuckling.

"Hey, I'm not stubborn....much," I say. "Gracie is the one. I know it, but I feel like she thinks I'm moving too fast. I know she feels it, too, but I worry that I'm being too pushy."

"There's a difference between being pushy and being determined. You can act with conviction and strength without being disrespectful of her feelings. Just remember to always be honest with her and never stop communicating your feelings," Dad says.

I've always respected my dad and looked up to him. He has a way of making everything clear. He seems to always have control over everything. I cringe when I think of how much the loss of control over me must have affected him. I never really thought about it or his feelings.

"Dad. I'm sorry for the way I left back then. I'm also sorry for staying away for so long. You know I never intended to hurt you or Mom, right?" I say with as much sincerity that I can muster.

"Ezekiel. You are my boy. We've been through this already. Stop beating yourself up about it. You are home now. Grab the girl and make a home with her. Give your Mom and me some grandbabies and all will be forgiven," he says grinning.

"Let me convince her to marry me first, Dad," I say, shaking my head.

When I get home, I see Gracie and Akia curled up and asleep on the couch. I laugh when I see the empty containers of ice cream on the coffee table.

They both stir awake and Akia announces that she needs to head home. Gracie immediately gets up and starts cleaning up the mess, avoiding making eye contact. I'm not sure what that's all about. Her emotions have been all over the place lately.

I head up to get ready to bed and see a line of pregnancy tests on the bathroom counter. Picking one of them up, I see it's positive and immediately yell out, "Babe, what the fuck is this?"

Gracie appears in the doorway with a shocked look on her face. "Akia is pregnant." I say, looking back down at the tests. That's got to be it. It would explain the indulgence in ice cream.

"Well, yeah actually she is," Gracie says looking at her feet. "But those aren't hers."

"Wait. What?" I say, feeling my heart beat increase in speed.

"Those aren't hers," she repeats, looking up with a shy smile on her face.

I immediately rush over to her and pull her into my arms. "Are you saying what I think you are saying? But you are on the pill. Did you miss a day? Or do I have super sperm? Please tell me I have super sperm because that would be the most awesome thing I could hear right now. Besides hearing that I'm going to be a fucking dad. Holy shit. I'm going to be a fucking dad," I say, sweeping Gracie up in my arms and walk her across the hall to the bedroom.

Gracie is giggling against my neck and places a soft kiss against my jaw. "Just like you, your sperm must have ninja skills. I never missed a day. Are you okay with this? I mean I know we've talked about it jokingly, but it's no longer a joke. This is real. We are going to have a baby, Zeke. Shit, I don't know if I'm ready for this,"

"Super sperm! I knew it. Sweet girl, I couldn't be happier. Yeah, it wasn't planned, but obviously, it is meant to be. I mean, I love you. You are my future. This baby is a miracle in a sense. It just makes it more real that we are meant to be," I say, setting her down on the bed and dropping to my knees.

I place my hand against her stomach and look up at her beautiful face. I feel my throat start to choke up, and I feel like my eyes are starting to well up with tears.

Running her thumbs under my eyes, I see a tear roll down her cheek. "I love you so much. I knew something was off, but never did I think it was this. Akia and I are going to be fat and cranky together."

"So, she is really pregnant too?" I ask.

"Yeah, she told me at dinner and asked me to be the baby's godmother. As we were talking, things started rolling through my head, the same with Akia. I took the tests just to get her to be quiet about it all, never thinking it would be true," she says, placing her hand over top of mine.

"You need to be careful at work. I don't want you to be lifting heavy shit anymore. Make an appointment so you can get on those vitamins that pregnant women take," I say, standing up and starting to pace.

"Zeke, please don't be like Doug. Akia says she can barely take a shit without him trying to look in on her," she laughs.

"I knew I liked him. I'm going to apologize now for my over protectiveness. But not only do I have you to worry about, I now have my kid in there. We can still have sex though, right? Because my testosterone is off the charts right now just thinking I beat the odds and got you pregnant. I mean, look I'm hard as a rock here, babe," I say, pointing at my crotch. She starts laughing and shaking her head. "Hey, it's a man thing. I can't help it."

"Yes, we can have sex. I think I would die if we couldn't. I've been thinking about it all day, for the past week. It's like I can't get enough," she says as she stands and starts quickly peeling off her clothes.

"Beautiful," I say, mimicking her as I start taking off my clothes just as fast.

We make slow, passionate love. I pour everything I can into my touches and kisses. This beautiful woman is carrying my child. I can't believe how lucky I am to have found my soulmate. I fall asleep with the woman I love in my arms and a smile on my face.

# CHAPTER EIGHTEEN
## *Giving Thanks*

## ZEKE

The women have both kitchens going full steam. The men are all sitting around the living room, drinking beers, and watching football. I know I sound like a broken record, but I can't believe I opted out of experiencing this all those years. I made a couple of Thanksgivings, don't get me wrong, but this one just seems more significant.

I know I can't say anything about Gracie being pregnant yet. We found out that she's four week's along, which means my super sperm pretty much hit the target on the first try. I was worried that her taking the pill the whole time would be bad for the baby, but the doctor reassured us that everything would be fine.

I have the grainy black and white photo tucked in my wallet. My baby. It looked like nothing but a bean, but it was the most beautiful thing I've ever seen in my life. Except for the smile on Gracie's face. If I can't make the announcement about the baby yet, I plan on making up for it.

Doug keeps giving me knowing glances and smiles. I guess Akia let the cat out of the bag and he knows. I'm kind of glad that he does, at least I have someone I can talk to that's going through the same thing right now.

We hear an announcement that the food is ready. All of us get up and head into the dining room. We have tables lined up through to the kitchen. I look through the dining room through the kitchen and see that the mud room door is open. There's a table set up in view where all the kids are getting into seats.

Dad clears his throat and gets little response. He finally whistles loudly and the whole house and apartment go quiet. We bow our heads and hold hands as he says grace. The moment "Amen"' ring out, the buzz of voices are raised once again.

We are all finished and just sitting around talking. I take this opportunity to make my move. I stand and ask for everyone's attention.

Taking Gracie's hand in mine, I pull her up to her feet. "Gracie Lynn Murray. I know it seems like we've just met, but as my dad says, when you know, you know. I loved you the moment I scared the shit out of you that first day. When you looked up at me, you literally knocked the breath out of me with those soft sky blue eyes."

Reaching into my front pocket, I pull out a ring and get down on one knee. "Will you do me the honors of saying you will be my wife, my partner, the mother of my children and make me the happiest man on this earth? Marry me?" I ask.

"Oh my God Zeke. I...can't...wow...you are full of surprises. Of course, I will marry you," she says, holding out her left hand and letting me slip the ring on her finger.

I stand and pull her into my arms as cheers of congratulations fill the house.

# GRACIE

When Zeke stood up and got everyone's attention, I started to get mad. He promised that he wouldn't say anything. It's too early. Then he gets down on one knee and blows me away. He proposed. I'm still in shock as I look down at the brilliant diamond sitting on my finger.

I can still see the smile on my dad's face. I'm so glad he was here to experience this with me.

The men all retire to the living room to continue to watch football. The women clean up and put away all the leftovers. Each of them come over and look at the ring and ooh and ahh over it.

Akia and I set out all the desserts and ask if any of the guys want any. We see a few hands go into the air and I laugh that they are so into the game on the TV.

We put some goodies onto plates and carry them in, handing them out. I'm pulled into Zeke's lap and feel him press his groin into my backside. I'm wondering if it's possible for us to sneak away for a quickie as I grind down on him.

I grab the plate out of his hand and take a big forkful to disguise my moan. Handing the plate back, I stand and quickly run up the stairs, looking at Zeke and smiling.

He looks around and sees that everyone is so into the game and not paying attention. He quickly stands and sets his plate on the coffee table following me up the steps.

"We have to be quick and quiet," I say, pushing my tights down my legs and bending over the bed.

Zeke pushes the door shut and locks it, undoing his pants and pushing them down over his ass. He's completely erect and I can almost see it pulsing.

There's no time for foreplay, I'm soaking wet anyways and am ready for him. I feel him enter me in one thrust as I slam back against him. With his hands digging into my hips, he pounds in and out of me, and I can quickly feel myself starting to fall over the edge. Zeke reaches around me and starts rubbing my clit which makes me see stars. Within seconds, I'm grunting out my orgasm as quietly as I can as I feel him swell inside of me, grunting out his release.

"Damn I needed that, sweet girl," Zeke says, pulling out and grabbing a dirty shirt to wipe me off.

"You can say that again. I think I need a nap now though. Turkey and sex is a deadly combination," I laugh, pulling my leggings back up.

"I love you. Promise me that this will be a tradition every Thanksgiving, hell every holiday, every party. Such a turn on to know we have a house full of people," he says, taking me into his arms and giving me a sweet kiss.

As we descend the steps, Bradley looks back over the couch at us throwing a thumbs up. "Pulled a Bradley, huh? Damn I miss those. Tell your Aunt Carrie I need to see her quick."

I can feel my face heating up and I'm sure I'm blushing. Zeke kisses my temple and smacks my ass as I hurry away to get out of the living room and away from humored faces.

◆◆◆

I'm exhausted. It took me everything to remain awake until ten. I didn't want to add any suspicion and head to bed before all the guests were gone. So, I stuck with it and powered through. You know how hard it is to accomplish this on no caffeine? I don't know how I'm going to make it through eight more months of no coffee.

I crash into bed and curl under the covers and Zeke follows behind, pulling me into his front. He kisses my shoulder and I snuggle into him closer.

"My dad told me you asked him for permission to marry me. He said that even though he didn't know you very well, he knew your family. Plus, the fact that you even asked for his permission, he was impressed. He also said that he could tell that I was happy. That I almost glowed. I swear he knows I'm pregnant. He just had this smile and look on his face. It took everything in me not to blurt it out. He looked truly happy. It's been a long time since I've seen that kind of happiness on his face. Thank you," I say, looking back and kissing Zeke's nose.

"I'm so thankful this Thanksgiving. Thankful that you said yes, that I was able to score this beautiful woman who is now carrying my child. I'm thankful that I'm home and got to experience this with you and my family," Zeke says, cradling my stomach. "Sleep, my sweet girl. I love you."

"I love you, too. Thank you for being mine. I'm truly blessed to have such a wonderful man in my life," I say, snuggling and quickly falling to sleep.

## ZEKE

I lay there for a while and just listen to her sleep. My arm is falling asleep from being under her head, but I can't move. I don't want to move. I love feeling her in my arms. I think back over this day and smile.

Watching football with the guys in my family is nothing less than hilarious. None of the teams that were playing were any of our teams, but we all picked sides. Not always the same one either. This made for some crazy bets and taunting and gloating.

Uncle Bradley has always secretly been my favorite uncle. I mean, he's funny and a really cool guy. He's never hidden any of his feelings for Uncle Bruce or Aunt Carrie from us. So, needless to say, the bets that he and Uncle Bruce were making were causing even me to blush.

Before dinner, I had asked Gracie's dad if we could talk. I wanted to ask his permission to marry her. At the end of the conversation, we were both smiling and even gave each other a hug. I had his permission, which I was grateful for.

I get up the next morning and make my famous omelet. I brew a pot of decaf coffee. The sacrifices I'm willing to make for my girl. I put everything on a tray and head up the stairs. I see the bathroom door closed and set the tray down on a table in the hallway.

"Gracie, everything okay?" I ask, knocking lightly on the door.

I get a soft, "Morning sickness" as a reply. I ask if she needs me and I get a response of no and that she will be out in a few minutes. I look down and the food and grimace. I don't think she's going to want to eat.

I'm still standing there staring at the food when the door opens. "Oh my God, you cooked me breakfast? Your omelet too? Babe, that's so sweet."

"Sorry, I'll get it out of here, I'm sure you probably don't want to eat right now," I say going to pick up the tray.

"Absolutely not. I'm good now and actually starving," she says, picking up the tray and walking into the bedroom.

I follow behind her laughing at how she has a death grip on the tray. She scoots into the bed not spilling a thing. "Please tell me this is decaf," she says, raising the cup to her nose and taking in a deep smell.

"I would never torture you like that, sweet girl, of course it's decaf. I know it won't give you that kick, but at least you can indulge in the taste," I say, crawling in bed beside her.

"Please God, let me keep this down. I'm starving," she says, taking a little sip and letting out a moan. "Oh, how I've missed you. I know you have no juice, but the taste is oh so good. I'll pretend you are loaded."

I watch as she takes another sip and waits to see if she will keep it down. With a smile, she picks up a fork and takes a small bite of the omelet. I continue to watch as she slowly chews and swallows. She shrugs her shoulders and continues to eat.

Getting that she's not going to be sick, I grab a fork and take a few bites myself. We make it through the omelet with success. The smile she gives me when I set the tray to the side is one that I will always remember.

There are moments in my life with her that are profound. The first time we met eyes. The first date and hearing her sweet voice. Looking into her window and seeing her put on a little show for me. The moment I entered her and felt her lose herself to me. When I found out that I was going to be a dad, to her saying yes to being my wife. Yet the simple little smile that I get from her today is stored away as a treasured moment. I vow to make sure she has a reason to give me that smile every day for the rest of our lives.

# CHAPTER NINETEEN

*Christmas in New York*

## ZEKE

I got a call from my sister Destiny saying that she didn't think that she was going to make it for Christmas. She lives in Long Island with her husband and three kids. One biologically and the other two adopted brother and sister.

Destiny went through a traumatic event in her childhood. In the end, she ended up with my mom and dad and grew into an amazing woman. She leads an advocacy for women of domestic violence, and I've always looked up to her and how she strives to give back so that others have the opportunity that she had.

She tells me about her plan to have a pretty big event that sounds like it's bigger than the Salvation Army Christmas Tree that I've participated in every year. I ask if there is anything I can do to help and she immediately starts rattling off things.

"Do you think you and Gracie can really make it? It's right before Christmas, so you won't miss out on doing your own thing. I would love to have you here," she says with excitement.

"Destiny. You are amazing. I would be honored to be a part of this. Let me talk to Gracie and see what we can do," I say.

"Perfect. Let me know. I know the kids will be excited to see you. I hope you can make it. Love you," she says.

"Love you, too, sis, talk soon," I say, ending the call.

I walk out to the stables and find Gracie and tell her about the conversation that I had with Destiny.

"Oh wow, that sounds amazing. I would love to go and meet her. I've always heard so many good things about her. To give something back, I would be honored. I'm sure William will be fine with it. I've reduced my hours anyways and it's only one or two days, right?" she asks.

"Yeah, I'm thinking we leave on Friday and come back on Monday. Just so it's not rushed. I'm really excited about this. I've never seen her in her element. I've missed out on her kids, too. But I know how much this means to her. To be a part of it, finally...I'm really pumped," I say, giving her a hug and a kiss.

## GRACIE

William has to be the best boss ever, or he just understands the value of family. He doesn't blink an eye at my request to have off. I've always admired the diversity and love that this family displays. They have no idea of how inspirational they are, I believe this. As an outsider, I've always been in awe at the amount of love and acceptance they have shown.

It's the weekend before our trip, so I talked Zeke into going Christmas shopping for his sister's family.

I put him in charge of buying for Jeremy, Destiny's husband, and his nephew Dawson. I take the girls, of course. The oldest is fifteen and I'm a little nervous on what to buy a girl that age. The youngest is ten, which is also a hard age. They can play with dolls one minute and think they are ready for makeup the next.

I find a couple of holiday scented candles and a beautiful cashmere scarf for Destiny. I'm standing in the middle of the mall looking between a tchotchke trinket type jewelry store and a makeup store. I must look lost because a woman and her daughter walk up and stand beside me.

"What are the ages?" the woman asks.

"Sorry?" I say. "Oh, do I look that confused? Umm, one is fifteen and the other in ten, and I've never met them."

"Hard ages," she laughs as I nod my head looking at her for any insight she can provide.

I'm guessing it's her daughter who takes my hand and says, "I'm twelve. That's about exactly in between the two. I don't sit on Santa's lap anymore, so maybe this will help me get the gift I really want." Laughing, I let her lead me into the jewelry store.

"Okay, so these are really popular right now. You can make your own necklaces and bracelets. The cool thing about them is you can continue to buy add on packages. I suggest the starter pack and maybe one add on. This is for the ten-year-old, by the way," she says, picking up a starter pack and taking a second to look over the add on packages.

I go and pay and the daughter grabs my hand and leads me over to the makeup store. Her mom is smiling the whole time and I'm just grateful that, somehow, I was blessed to meet this child.

She leads me over to a section that looks like it's made just for teenagers. I'm in awe at the selections.

"Now, the older girls are into all these online makeup tutorials. Contouring and all that stuff. So, for the fifteen-year-old, I suggest getting her one of these kits. It even comes with a list of the online tutorials that promote this product to help her with the application. Even if she's not allowed to wear makeup yet, which would just be totally unrealistic, she can at least try it at home," she says, shrugging her shoulder and giving her mom a look.

I'm cracking up laughing at this amazing kid who I finally learn is Jessica. "Yeah, right. Nothing wrong with trying it out a home, right mom?" I say, looking at her mom who just shakes her head and smiles.

"Jessica, thank you so much for noticing a woman in shear desperation. I couldn't have done it without you. I see a job as a personal shopper in your future," I say, giving her and her mom a hug.

I'm holding my packages and asking them if I can treat them to ice cream when Zeke walks up and wraps his arms around me and kisses my temple.

"Wow, is that your boyfriend? He's cute!" Jessica says and then blushes. "Sorry did I just blurt that out loud?"

I introduce them and tell Zeke how Jessica was such a help to me today. They pass on the offer of ice cream but we exchange numbers. I didn't really get a chance to talk with the mom, but if her daughter is that awesome, she has to be as well.

# ZEKE

Another road trip. I actually love road trips with Gracie. There is never a dull moment. Even when she falls asleep, I'm giving the privilege of watching her. I just can't believe how beautiful she is and she is all mine.

She captures videos of me singing. Every moment is documented for her little blog. It's like the old-time home movies that we will pull together and show our kids and grandkids one day.

We make it to my sister's house in record time. We grab the presents out of the truck and are greeted at the door by Jeremy.

"Did you have a good trip? No issues?" Jeremy asks, letting us in the door.

"No issues, the traffic wasn't bad at all. I think we came through at a good time of the day," I say, setting the presents at my feet and giving him a man hug. "Jeremy, this is my fiancé Gracie."

Jeremy is a good foot taller than I am and I laugh as Gracie stands there cranking her head back to look at him. "You're Jeremy Winters."

Laughing, Jeremy says, "That would be my name, yes."

"Zeke, it's Jeremy Winters. Why didn't you tell me?" she exclaims.

"I didn't think you would know who he even was to be honest," I say.

"I watch sports. I may not be a huge basketball fan, but I know who Jeremy Winters is for goodness sake," she says still staring up at him. "Wow, okay Gracie stop looking like a star struck idiot. Um, I hate to be rude, but I really need to use the restroom."

"Sure thing, right down the hall the first door on your right is a powder room," Jeremy says as Gracie takes off practically running. "Your girl is funny. I have to say I've never had that reaction before."

Smiling, I say, "She has a tendency to ramble when she's nervous. I seriously didn't think she would even know who you were, no offense."

"None taken. Come in and get comfortable. Destiny is finalizing some things for the event and should be home soon. Kids will be home from school soon as well. It's good to have you here. Destiny has been really excited to see you both," Jeremy says, leading me into the living room.

Gracie joins us a few minutes later and seemed to have regained her normalcy around Jeremy. It's not long before the kids come storming into the house. There's backpacks flying and they are all trying to talk at once.

When they finally realize Gracie and I are there, they shout "Uncle Zeke" in unison. I introduce them to Gracie and tell them she will be their Aunt soon. They start calling her Auntie Grace almost immediately. This creates a smile on Gracie's face that fills my heart.

Destiny comes home and immediately pulls me into a hug. I've missed her hugs so much. We stand and hug for what seems like five minutes and I almost get choked up.

Pizza is ordered and devoured and presents are exchanged and opened. I believe that Gracie has won the award of favorite aunt with her choice of gifts.

It seems the whole family is placing Gracie in high regard. I'm okay with that, since I hold her in high regard, too. She just has something about her that is easy to love.

The next morning, we all pile into Destiny's SUV and head into the city. There's a Boy's and Girl's Club that is in a fairly large building. Several clubs got together to join in this event. Admission is free to any club member and their families and there are several things going on for all the kids.

Jeremy and some of his old NBA buddies are playing basketball with some of the older teens. I somehow got signed up to be the entertainment. I had a feeling this was going to happen, so I placed a call to Lee who came through and showed up with the band. You should have seen the eyes on everyone when they all walked through the door.

One mini concert later and tons of junk food, someone dressed in a Santa suit comes out followed by a bunch of people dressed as elves carrying big red satchels. I laugh when I notice that Gracie is one of those elves. It feels so wrong that I'm totally turned on right now. I wonder if she can keep the outfit.

## GRACIE

I'm drifting around helping out where I can, but I don't feel like I'm doing enough. Destiny pulls me aside and says she needs help with the next event, but it means I have to dress in an elf suit. At first, I think that I'm too big to fit in an elf costume, but surprisingly the material is stretchy and I think I look pretty damn good. We haven't said anything about the pregnancy, but I'm worried about carrying heavy objects, so after getting changed, I pull Destiny aside.

"Oh my God, you look adorable," she says smiling.

"Thanks. Umm, we didn't want to say anything just yet, but I think I need you to know that I'm pregnant," I say, looking down at my feet.

"Oh...wow...that's wonderful! I'm going to be an aunt. I'm so excited for you guys. Okay, I'll make sure you get the light packages. So, am I the only one that knows?" she says with a huge smile on her face.

"Well, Akia knows. She's the one that forced me to take the damn test, even though I thought there was no way I could be pregnant. I was on the pill and never missed a day. She's pregnant, too, and got it in her head that we could be pregnant together and stuff. Turned out she was right. But other than that, yes, you are the only one that knows," I say.

"Yes! I love it when I have inside information. I don't know if you know this, but our family can be somewhat competitive. Especially Uncle Bradley. I can't wait to tell him I knew the whole time," she says, pulling me in for a hug. "I'm happy for you. I can tell that you really love Zeke and that he loves you. Hell, the short time I've been around you, I think I love you, too."

Laughing I say, "Yeah, I love you, too, and your family."

We all head out behind Santa and I can feel his eyes on me. I look over and see Zeke adjust himself. He has that look on his face as he looks me up and down. It feels like he is undressing me with his eyes. I instantly feel myself grow wet. A simple look and I'm done.

I don't know how she pulled it off, but every kid there got a present. She had them labeled gender and age specific. These weren't dollar store items either. We are talking Kindles and Xbox consoles. I was amazed. The kids were almost in shock when they opened them.

I have to say this was one of the best days I've ever experienced. I can't believe how good I feel just being a part of this. I tried to see if I could keep the costume, but they were rentals and needed to be returned. I'll have to see if I can get myself a sexy one to role play with. I can only imagine how Zeke would react.

We get back to the house and say our goodnights. Zeke and I go to the quest bedroom, and I instantly crash into bed. I feel him crawl behind me and pull me close.

"You looked really sexy in that elf costume," Zeke says, kissing the back of my head.

"I could tell. I'll get one, promise," I say, cuddling down.

"Good. I love you, sweet girl," he responds.

"I love you, too. Forever," I respond.

"Forever sounds good to me," he says as his breathing gets heavier.

I fall asleep in the arms of the man I love. The one that I see always in my future.

# CHAPTER TWENTY

*Wedding Plans*

## ZEKE

"We never talked about when to get married. Do you want to get married before or after the baby is born?" I ask as we drive back home.

"Well, I've always pictured both a big and a small wedding. I don't really care, Zeke. Just being your wife is what matters. I'd rather not be huge, but I'd really like to be married before the baby comes," she says with a shrug.

"So, let's make plans. I want this to be as special as I can make it. I don't want just a justice of the peace, wham bam kind of nuptials. I want as many of our family members as we can there to celebrate. Other than that, I don't really care either," I say, looking over and smiling.

"I'm a month along and won't start really showing for at least two or three more months. Can we pull something off that quick? With the holidays and everything?" she says.

"Let's call my mom. She pulled her and dad's off fairly quickly. I bet she'll jump right in and take care of things. Just make sure you keep tabs on her, she can be a bit of a whirlwind," I say.

I hit the phone button on the steering wheel and hear the phone ringing through the speakers. Mom answers and I tell her our plan. Within minutes she has Gracie's favorite color and flower. She says that she will call their church to see what dates can be worked with and get back to us. She also suggests a local restaurant that has rooms you can rent for the reception and says she'll give them a call as well to see if there are coordinating dates to work with.

I hang up and pull Gracie's hand to my lips. "That was easy. Looks like we are getting married soon."

"I can't wait," she says, bouncing in her seat.

We are about an hour away from home when my mom calls us back. "January twenty-sixth. Both church and restaurant are being held upon confirmation and deposit. I called the florist that your dad gets my flowers from. Since we are their most frequent and loyal customers, they are giving us a discount. She can do fresh or silk gardenias and stargazer lilies. Silk will be cheaper and quicker to get in to work with. When are you going to be home?"

"Take a breath, Mom. We will be home in about an hour." I look at Gracie, who is smiling as tears run down her face. "January twenty-sixth?"

"January twenty-sixth," she says, nodding her head and wiping the tears away.

"Got it. I'll confirm and take care of the deposit. Gracie, I'll be over tonight. We got this. Drive safe and see you both later," she says as the phone goes dead.

"Wow, you weren't kidding. Your mom is amazing," she says, pulling out her phone and marking the date on the calendar.

There's a buzz of excitement the rest of the ride home. Gracie called all her friends with the news. It makes me smile to hear her so happy.

## GRACIE

I feel like my head is spinning with all the thoughts rolling through it. I'm trying to mentally tick off the things I'm going to need to do before the wedding.

After talking with Akia, I think about what she said about her wedding. You do all this planning and in a blink, it's over. The only thing she really remembers is the food, friends, and family that were there. Oh, and her dress. So that's all I'm going to worry about. I don't care what the cake looks like. I don't care about anything but becoming Mrs. Gracie Boyd. So, I'm going to make sure all my friends and family know the date and times and figure out my dress. Since Jamie was able to secure the restaurant, we'll just need to go over the menu and that will be done. I've gone to receptions there before, so I know they already have the twinkling lights and nice decorations, so I'm not worried about any of those details.

Speaking of dresses. I always thought that I would alter my mom's wedding dress and wear it for mine. She was built exactly like me, so I'm hoping nothing much will need done.

I always loved her dress. It was simple silk with a sweetheart cut but had lace across the chest and down the arms. The back has a deep v exposing almost the entire back area. It's elegant and I've always pictured myself in it one day. I call my dad to give him a heads up to pull it down from the attic and let him know he has to cancel any plans that day so he can walk me down the aisle. I can hear him choke up a bit when he responds that nothing would stop him from missing it.

I can feel the tears start to well up as I disconnect the call. I feel Zeke place his hand on my shoulder and squeeze. "You okay?" he asks.

"Just sad thinking about my mom not being here. I could hear Dad's voice crack a bit. I want to wear her dress, but I'm second guessing myself. I don't want to make him sad. Emotions are going to be running high as it is for both of us," I say, leaning my cheek against his hand.

He runs his thumb under my eye attempting to wipe the tears that continue to flow. "Talk to him about it first before you change your mind. I mean, this is going to be one of the happiest days of my life. I'm sure that was one of his, too, when he married your mom. It may bring back happy and good memories. If it means that much to you, I'm sure he will understand. You may be surprised with his reaction, or you will at least know for sure and not think back and have any regrets that you didn't ask."

"There you go with your wise and sweet words. Thank you. I'll talk to him about it when I go try on the dress. Who knows, it may not even fit or be capable of being altered if it doesn't." I wipe my face and blow my nose and then lean across the truck, scratching his beard and giving him a kiss.

As we pull into our driveway, Jamie pulls in right beside us. "Perfect timing, damn I'm good," she says getting out of her Volkswagen. For as long as I've known her, that's the only type of car she has owned.

She pulls out a big binder that has tabs that appear to already to be written on. Walking towards the house, she looks back at me and says, "Get a move on, young lady, we've got a wedding to plan."

Jamie had menus printed off from the restaurant and Zeke and I quickly marked the things we wanted. She then flips to the next tab with pictures of wedding cakes.

"Oh my God. How did you pull this off so quickly?"

"Sweetie, I'm an activities director remember, and even though you may not think so, we have actually had a few weddings at the living facility. Plus, I've been dabbling in cake decorating. These are actually ones that I have done. If you don't like any of these, I'm sure I can make one you do like," she says proudly.

"Wow, umm, I really like this one, but can I have stargazer lilies down and around instead?" I ask.

"Of course. Is there anything else you would want to change?" she says, marking a big circle around the picture.

"No, it's perfect and beautiful. You are really talented," I say. "What are the other tabs for?"

"Dress shops, which I understand we don't need. Invitation ideas, which we may need to discuss since this is a quick turnaround. I'm thinking we do quick postcards that direct your guests to a web site that I'll help get set up, and they can reply with whether they can make it or not. We can also email them instead with a link to the website or both. Do you have an idea of who you are going to invite? I'll need an estimated head count to make sure we have enough room at the restaurant," Jamie says.

"I'll be happy with just close friends and family. Off the top of my head, I'm thinking around thirty on my side," I say and look at Zeke.

"Let's make it seventy-five for now then, just to be safe," Zeke says.

At this point, everything is mostly planned. I can't believe it. We still have work to do, but in one evening, Jamie has it all organized and ready. I'm in awe and totally exhausted.

We fall into bed together and Zeke worships every inch of my body, sending me over the edge twice. I don't even remember falling asleep, but I know I was smiling when I did.

The next morning I'm awoken by the smell of omelet and coffee. Zeke has again brought me breakfast in bed. "You are going to spoil me by doing this all the time," I say, sitting up and setting the tray on my lap.

"My sweet girl. It is my job to spoil you. I want nothing more than to be the reason you smile every second of every day," he says, crawling into bed and grabbing a fork full of eggs.

"You don't have to do anything special to make me smile. I smile every day knowing that I'm carrying your child and will soon be your wife," I say smiling. "Damn, that sounded really mushy. Maybe we should write a romance novel about us."

"It would be a hell of a story. I know I'd read it," he says laughing. "It was a bit mushy, but if it's honest, that's all that matters. I love you, sweet girl."

"I love you, too. I'm going to put in a few hours on the farm and then head over to Dad's after. What do you have planned today?" I ask.

"I'm going to go ask people to be in my wedding. I'm a little lost on who to have as my best man, though, on such short notice. I mean I have friends, but I can't say that I have a best friend. Pretty sad when I think about it. I thought about just asking my dad. He's everything to me. Yet, I thought about Lee and even Jeremy. I have no clue what to do," Zeke says.

I start running my hand over his bald head and say, "I know how much you look up to your dad. There's nothing wrong if you choose him. Yet, I saw the connection that you and Lee have. There's something special there too. As for Jeremy, there's a connection between you two as well. I say if they can, they should all be in the wedding party. Honestly, I'm sort of in the same situation. I want Akia to be my matron of honor, of course. Other than that, I have no clue who else to ask. Would it be strange to have your mom and

Destiny as part of the wedding? If we do that, then it would make more sense to have Lee as your best man, that way the wives can be paired up together with their husbands. Or we can just forgo anyone else and just do matron of honor and best man."

"It's a small wedding. I think we should do that. I'll see if I can get Lee and we'll keep it at that. You say I have wise words of wisdom, but I think you do, too. Communication. Sometimes that is all is needed to work things out. Thank you, babe," he says, looking at his phone. I'm sure he's trying to decide if it's too early to call Lee.

"Call him. I'll bet he will answer even it's early. If he does, you know you made the right choice," I say, setting the tray aside and heading to the bathroom to get ready for work.

I'm in the shower and hear the door open and close. The shower curtain moves and Zeke steps inside with me. I feel his hardness against my ass and instantly start grinding against him. He pushes lightly on my shoulders and I plant my hands flat against the wall bending over. No words are spoken as I feel him slide slowly inside of me. It never ceases to amaze me on how incredible he feels each time. With one hand on my shoulder and one hand on my hip, he starts to pick up speed. He's pulling me back as he pushes forward. The only sound is of our bodies slapping together and the groans that continue to grow louder. He makes my whole body come to life. I feel him swell and I'm pushed over the edge the same time he releases inside of me.

"Love you, sweet girl," he says, holding me close and kissing my temple.

"Love you, too, beast," I say laughing.

"Lee answered and said he would be honored, so it's done. I'm taking your advice and leaving it at that," he say, giving me another kiss.

"I had a feeling that was how it was going to go. It's going to be perfect," I sigh.

"It already is," he says.

I put in a few hours on the farm helping William in the office. I ended up tell him about the pregnancy, and he immediately gave me more office responsibilities. Seems he's just as protective as Zeke. He doesn't even want me in the barn or stables any longer. Which sucks, I love those horses.

I think word is going to travel quickly, so I'm going to tell my dad tonight and getting Zeke to invite his parents over to dinner so we can tell them and Pam. I thought about having dad come, too, so we could announce it all at once, but tonight is my dad's bowling night.

I know I will only have a few hours if I don't get over there now. I call Zeke to tell him my plan and to see if his parents can make it on such short notice. He wanted to go with me, but I told him if the dress did work out, it was bad luck for him to see me in it. He pouted for a few minutes, but eventually gave in.

I get to my dad's and walk in to see him standing in the living room, staring at the box that my mom's dress is in.

"Dad, are you alright?" I say.

"Marrying your mom was one of the happiest days of my life, Gracie Lynn. I'm a little nervous to see that dress again," he says, looking over his shoulder at me with a sad smile.

"Oh Dad, I was worried about that. I don't have to wear it if it's going to cause you any pain," I say, wrapping my arms around his belly and hugging him from behind.

"You will wear it if you can. You've always looked at our wedding pictures and said you would, even when your mom was alive. I know she will be looking down on you and be smiling. I wouldn't want to piss your mom off by being the reason you don't wear it. I can almost feel her slapping me in the back of the head," he says with a soft chuckle and patting my arms.

I hesitantly release him from the hug and walk around him. Sitting down on the couch, I run my hand over the sealed box.

"Help me open it?" I ask.

He pulls out a pocket knife and sits down beside me. Carefully he cuts the tape as I slowly open the lid. I can feel the tears start to flow down my face. "It's still beautiful."

"Go try it on. Let's see it," Dad says as he stands.

Pulling the dress carefully out of the box, I fold it over my arm and go into the den. I shut the door and hang it on the back and take a few minutes to just look it over. I can see my mom wearing it just like in the pictures and smiling at me.

Taking a deep breath and blowing it out, I undress. I'm now scared that it's not going to fit. I'm pacing back and forth biting my bottom lip.

"Okay, Gracie, just do it," I whisper to myself.

Pulling the dress off the delicate hanger, I unzip and unbutton the back. I close my eyes as I step into it. Putting my arms through the lace sleeves, I pull each side up on my shoulders. I reach behind me and slowly raise the zipper to the small of my back. It closed without issue. I take another cleansing breath and look into the mirror that's attached to the back of the door.

At first, I see my mom looking back at me, then slowly see that it's me. I didn't realize how much I looked like her until now. It fits. In fact, it fits so well, I don't think I'll need alterations at all. I just hope there is room for the added baby weight I will undoubtedly gain over the next month.

I slowly open the door to see my dad on the other side. "Oh wow. It's a perfect fit. You look just as stunning as your mom did all those years ago. I'm so proud of you. You are going to wear it, right?"

"I can't imagine wearing any other dress. Especially now that I see myself in it," I say, running my hands down the front and sides.

"I can take it to the cleaners for you and keep it here so Zeke doesn't see it, if you'd like," Dad says.

"Thank you, that would be perfect. Let me get changed. I know you have bowling tonight, but I want to talk to you about something beforehand," I say stepping back and closing the door.

One obstacle completed. I stand and stare at myself in the mirror for a few more minutes. Before I take off the dress, I take a quick photo. I gently put the dress back on the hanger and put it on the hook on the back of the door.

Dad is sitting on the couch holding a photo. I see that it's him and Mom. He gives me that gentle soft smile and pats the couch next to him.

I sit down and lean my head against his shoulder and look down at the photo. "I feel her smiling down on us right now. I know she sees us. I'm so happy the dress fits. I can't wait to walk you down the aisle. I'm surprised how fast this all happened, but I can tell you that I knew the moment I met your mom that she was my forever. I miss her every day."

"I do, too, Dad. You know that when I put on the dress and looked in the mirror, I swear it was her looking back at me. Smiling," I say, looking up at him.

"You look a lot like her. I'm happy for that. My little girl is a beautiful reminder of the love we shared," he says, tapping my nose with his finger.

"Dad I need to tell you something…you are going to be a grandfather," I say and rush to continue. "It's not the reason why we are getting married, but sort of the reason why we don't want to wait. I want to be married before the baby comes, and I don't want to be big as a whale when we do. It's a miracle really. I know you probably don't want details, but I was on reliable protection."

"Wow. I'm going to be a Pap. I knew something was different with you. I just thought it was just you being extremely happy," he says, pulling me in for hug.

"Well I am extremely happy, too," I say laughing. "I wanted to tell you since I had to tell William to explain why I couldn't do certain things on the farm. It's only a matter of time until word gets out, and I wanted you to hear it from me."

It's getting about time for him to head off to bowling, so we say our goodbyes. I take one more look at the picture I took in Mom's dress and drive home.

## ZEKE

I see the smile on her face as she comes in the door and instantly know. "It fit," I say smiling.

"It fit," she says, dancing in place.

"That's fantastic. I can't wait to see you in it," I says.

"Is Pam in our kitchen cooking? I smell something good," Gracie says, giving me a hug and a kiss.

"Yeah, I invited her over for dinner, and she kind of just took over. I know when not to interfere when it comes to her cooking," I respond. "My mom and dad will be here soon. Everything okay with your dad?"

"Really good. He said that I needed to wear the dress, Mom would have wanted it. We had a really good conversation and I believe he was overjoyed at the thoughts of being, as he called it, a Pap," she says, scratching my beard.

I love when she does that. I love to feel her touch, but it's like a thing of ours when she scratches the beard. I don't think I will ever shave it, just because of the feelings she stirs in me when she runs her fingers through it.

My mom and dad show up and we all take our seats at the table. Pam may be old, but the girl still has it. Everything looks incredible. My dad takes charge as he normally does and says the prayer as we all hold hands. I get a flash of memory of me as a kid with Destiny sitting around our table doing this exact same thing. I never thought of it as special back then, but now, it means so much to me.

We start eating and my leg is bouncing. "Mom, Dad... and of course Gram Pam...we have some news that we want to share."

I see my mom set her fork down and look to my dad for what I understand now as his direction.

"It's a miracle really. Totally not planned, but completely welcomed. We are pregnant...well Gracie is, but you know," I say, looking around the table at the reactions.

I see my mom cover her mouth with her hands and immediately stand up. "Oh my...Ezekiel. I'm going to be a Granny again? This is the best news ever!" She comes around that table and grabs both me and Gracie into an embrace.

Gram Pam is just sitting there with a look on her face that I can't interpret. I can't even look at my dad at this point because I'm too curious about her.

"Two babies," Gram Pam says "Akia and Gracie, I mean. I never thought I would live long enough to see all these great grandchildren. I was just thinking about Bill and how much he would have loved being a part of this."

Gracie immediately stands and goes over to give her a hug. "Him and my mom are staring down and smiling. They are here and see this, I just know it."

"Okay, enough sadness. Gracie, you are right. Let's eat and celebrate life and the joy of bringing a new one into the world," Gram Pam says, patting Gracie's arm.

I finally look at my dad and see his beaming smile. "I hope he turns out just like you. I'm proud of you, boy."

Laughing, I say "*He*, huh? What makes you sure it's going to be a boy?"

"You'll never understand how I feel until you have a boy of your own," he says chuckling.

# CHAPTER TWENTY-ONE

*Forever My Girl*

## ZEKE

The day quickly arrives and I'm a nervous wreck. I can't seem to get my stupid tie right. My dad steps over to me and grabs my hands.

"I got you. Let me. Take a deep breath. Damn, boy, you're sweating," Dad says, making a perfect Windsor knot.

"Were you this nervous with Mom?" I ask.

"I was nervous, but mostly excited. What are you so nervous about?" he asks.

"I don't know. I just want it to be perfect for her, I guess. She's here, right?" I say wiping the sweat off my smooth head.

"Yes, Ezekiel, of course, she's here. Your mom is with her and says Gracie is bouncing. Whatever that means," Dad says laughing.

A big smile forms on my face as I picture her doing that bouncing thing she always does when she is excited. My phone dings, so I pull it out of my pants pocket and swipe to unlock it.

Gracie: I'm so excited. I love you. See you soon.

I respond quickly.

Me: I love you so much. Can't wait to see you walk down that aisle.

Putting my phone back into my pocket, I feel a sense of calm come over me. It's like she knew that I needed to hear from her. Sometimes she amazes me. I'm so lucky to have found her.

We are summoned by the preacher, who says it's time. My dad gives me a big hug and a slap on the back and heads out. I follow him with Lee behind me.

Lee pats me on the back as we walk out into the church and take our places. It's just him and I at the front of the church. I see my mom sitting in the front pew with my dad, who just takes his seat next to her. She's already dabbing the tears from her eyes.

I look around the church and am met with smiles of all my family and close friends. There's a single white rose sitting on the opposite front pew of my parents. I know this is symbolic to represent Gracie's mom.

Music starts and the back doors open. Akia steps through and walks down the aisle. You can see her baby bump showing and she looks like she is glowing. Once she's in place, the music changes to the wedding march. I take a deep breath and blow it out.

I'm shifting from side to side in anticipation. I feel Lee place his hand on my shoulder to stop my movements. When I see Gracie and her dad step into view, my heart skips and starts pounding. I feel a lump form in my throat and I try to clear my throat. I look quickly to my feet and send up a prayer.

*Thank you, Heavenly Father, for bringing this beautiful woman into my life. I am forever grateful.*

I look back up and smile as I watch them walk down the aisle. She looks incredible. Her dress looks amazing on her. She has a small crown on her head with a small veil attached. Her hair is done like our first date, all in curls flowing down over her shoulders.

They make it in front of me and I can see her eyes are glistening, but her smile is huge. Her dad gives her a kiss on the cheek and places her hand in mine. We turn towards the minister but never break eye contact. I'm no longer nervous. I know this is my forever standing beside me. We both mouth the words I love you at the same time.

## GRACIE

I have the feeling my mom is hugging me as I slip into the dress. It feels a little tighter around my stomach, but when I look in the mirror, it's not very noticeable. I don't really care anyways.

Zeke's mom, Jamie, helps me put the small crowned vail made of crystals on the top of my head and secure it with hair pins. She gives me a kiss on the cheek and steps around to my front.

Squeezing my hands, she says, "You look simply gorgeous. I'm so proud to call you my daughter. Thank you for being the reason that Zeke finally came home. I had hoped he would one day, but I'm so happy that you are the reason why. I also can't wait for this little one to come into the world," she says, softly placing her hand on my stomach.

I start bouncing around the room in excitement. Jamie and Akia start laughing at my movements. Jamie steps out to talk to Zeke's dad, Sam, as I twirl around the room.

When she comes back in, she says that Sam told her that Zeke seemed nervous, but he had things under control.

"I'm not nervous at all," I say, grabbing my phone and sending Zeke a quick text telling him that I love him. Hopefully this will settle his nerves.

I get a quick response and smile. My dad pokes his head in the door and says that it's time. I grab my bouquet and lace my hand through my dad's arm.

I hear the music start from the other side of the door. Dad clears his throat and says, "Gracie Lynn. You look absolutely stunning in your mom's dress. I'm so happy for you and Zeke. Remember to always respect each other and never go to bed angry. Tell him you love him every single day, even if you are mad at him. Don't let one day go by without showing him how much you care about him. I love you very much. Let's go get you married."

After Akia makes her way down the aisle, Dad and I step into the doorway. My eyes connect with Zeke immediately. He looks incredible in his tux. He's shifting back and forth until I see Lee reach up and place his hand on his shoulder to stop him. I see him bow his head briefly and look back up meeting my eyes again.

I never take my eyes off his as we make it down the aisle. I can feel tears of happiness start to form in my eyes. My smile is so large I know my cheeks are going to hurt after this is over.

With a kiss on the cheek, my dad places my hand in Zeke's. We turn towards the preacher but never break eye contact. I giggle when we both mouth the words I love you at the same time.

We say our vows and exchange rings, continuing to keep eye contact. I can feel his love for me pouring off him. When the preacher says "You may now kiss the bride," Zeke takes my face in both hands and places a sweet kiss on my lips. At the announcement of presenting us as Mr. and Mrs. Ezekiel Boy, I throw my arm in the air.

We practically jog down the aisle. After greeting everyone, we step back in the church and take a few photos. We then exit as everyone throws bird seed as we race hand and hand to the limo.

We are the only ones riding inside, so I make sure the privacy glass is raised as I raise my dress and straddle Zeke's lap.

"I'm not waiting until tonight to consummate this marriage. I need you," I say, undoing Zeke's belt and pulling him out of his pants. He's already hard.

He leans around me and presses the intercom button. "Drive around until I pound on the glass, would you?"

Once he receives confirmation, he leans back and reaches under my dress. He softly kisses up my neck until he reaches my mouth and dives in. He slides my panties to the side and I guide him to my opening. I slide down on him as we continue to kiss. The movement of the limo causes us to shift around, but we never lose our rhythm.

"You feel so good, Mrs. Boyd," Zeke growls.

"You feel so good, too, Mr. Boyd," I moan.

I feel him swell and slam down on him and squeeze out my orgasm, throwing my head back and almost losing my veil. He squeezes my hips as he grinds up emptying inside of me.

We stay connected and press our foreheads together as we catch our breaths. "Don't clean up. I want to know I'm on you and in you the whole night," Zeke says.

I laugh as I slip off of him and get myself situated. Zeke does the same and knocks on the privacy glass. We pull up a few minutes later to the restaurant and walk in hand in hand. As we are greeted by the guests with clapping, we take our seats at the head table. Akia is snickering beside me, so I look over at her and ask what is so funny.

"Let me take off your veil, looks like it got a little crooked on your way over here," she says, reaching up and pulling out the hair pins.

"Oh God, how embarrassing," I say.

I look out to the guests just as Bradley holds up a wine glass and yells out, "You go, Z-man."

## ZEKE

Leave it to Uncle Bradley to notice Gracie's veil was crooked. I kiss her on the cheek to say I was sorry, but she just shrugs it and smiles. I know she's embarrassed by the glow on her cheeks, but my girl takes it in stride.

We get through dinner and Lee stands to give his speech. After getting everyone's attention, he lifts the mic and starts, "Good evening everyone. I can't tell you how honored I was to be asked by Zeke to be his best man. I first met Zeke when he was only eighteen years old, driving across the country on his way to Texas. During his time in Nashville, he helped me and my band out when one of our guitarist got sick. He has an amazing voice, if none of you realized or have heard him. We kept in touch over the years, and I got to see this young adventure seeking boy grow into an amazing man. When the band started to take off and get popular, I even ask him to join us on tour once. At this time in his life, he had finished college and was establishing himself into a really good job, so he declined. However, whenever we played in Texas, he always came to our shows.

"The first time I met Gracie, I knew instantly that these two we meant to be together forever. You could just see the love they had between them. It was almost tangible. Oh, and Gracie has a beautiful voice, too, by the way. I was thrilled to hear that they were getting married. When I hung up the phone, I turned to my wife and said, 'Told ya so.' I wish you two the best in what life has to offer you. I hope you are blessed with kids because you will make some beautiful children together. With that, please raise your glasses in a toast to the new Mr. and Mrs. Ezekiel Boyd."

Gracie and I stand and both give him a hug. "Thank you, that brought back a lot of memories," I say.

"It's not customary for the Maid or Matron of Honor to say anything, but I'd like to, if that's okay." Akia says into the mic.

I nod my head and she continues. "Zeke. Growing up we were inseparable. You were my best friend and protector…even when I didn't want you to be," she says smiling and making me laugh.

"Seriously people. It was a wonder I ever had a boyfriend in high school. But anyway, you've always been a special part of my life and my heart. It's a bond stronger than blood and I'm so grateful to be a part of this special day."

"Gracie. You are my girl. We've grown closer over this past year. I couldn't think of a better match than you for Zeke. The love oozes off the two of you. Thank you for bring him home," Akia drops the mic causing a screech and engulfs us in a hug.

I feel a lump in my throat when I feel her and Gracie both sniffing and laughing at the same time.

"Hormones," I say swallowing hard. "You know. You are the reason this all happened. If you wouldn't have broken my heart, things may have turned out differently and I would still be that miserable punk from back then."

"Nah. If it's meant to be it will be. You two are meant to be. You would have found each other eventually," she says kissing my cheek and stepping back.

I pull Gracie further in my arms and look into her eyes, "You are right. She's definitely meant to be,"

After gaining our composure, we go through the motions of cutting the cake that my mom made. I never realized how talented she was, the cake was incredible and tasted amazing. For our first dance, Lee sang us one of his songs he recently wrote called "Forever My Girl." We were the first to get to hear it and it was perfect.

We continue to dance and have a lot of fun, but I can tell that Gracie is starting to get tired. We say goodbye to our guests and I take us home. I carry her from the truck to the house and over the threshold. Using my foot, I close the door and proceed to carry her up the steps. I place her on the bed and help her out of her dress. Removing my clothes, I crawl into bed pulling her into my arm.

"I know you are exhausted, sweet girl. Go to sleep. I love you, wife," I say, cuddling in closer.

"I love you, husband," she says, pushing her head under my chin and kissing my chest.

I lay awake loving the feeling of her in my arms. I can't believe that she's my wife. It sounds so unreal. Reflecting back on how I got to today seems like a dream. I never thought that my journey in life would bring me right back to the place I thought I never wanted to be. But now I can't imagine being anywhere else.

We decided to wait to go on a honeymoon until after the baby is born. I want Gracie to be able to enjoy a frozen cocktail with the little umbrellas. If we can time it right, we may just go along with the family to the resort. Although she's not due until the end of July, it may not be this year we'd get to go, but I'd love to be able to be on the other side and enjoy everything as a guest. Gracie didn't really get to experience the full effect of the resort either. I'll have to run the idea by her. I fall asleep with the sweet smell of her hair and the pressure of her body half on me.

# CHAPTER TWENTY-TWO

*Baby Makes Three*

## ZEKE

Gracie gets bigger and bigger every day. I just love to watch the cute little waddle of her walk. We had our first argument and of all things it was over the color and decorations of the nursery. We found out that we are in fact, having a boy. I wanted to go camo and rustic, but she wanted baby blue with clouds and shit.

As you might guess, on the way to get the baby blue paint, I stopped and picked up flowers. I left angry that she wouldn't even hear me out, but then realized, it's a fucking color. Who really cares?

It's not important enough to have her upset over it, but I will have a discussion concerning how I feel. I want to at least be heard. It's the first time I've felt like my opinion didn't matter to her.

It's June and the temperature is starting to get hot. I know the heat is affecting Gracie, too. I mean I can't imagine what it would be like to be carrying a life inside you, plus, having to deal with hot temps.

I walk through the door carrying the cans of paint and flowers to see Gracie sitting on the couch crying. She jumps up and waddles over to me. Throwing her arms around my neck, she sobs out a sorry.

"Sweet girl, it's okay. It's only a color. I shouldn't have gotten so mad over it," I say, kissing her temple.

My hands are still full so I can't move or hug her back. She steps back and allows me to put the cans down. I extend my hand with the flowers and she smiles but ignores them and folds herself into my arms.

"I didn't mean to not listen to what you wanted. I just got this image in my head and didn't want you to talk me out of it. After you left, I realized how selfish I was being. This is your son, too. I'm sorry," Gracie says doing her normal tuck of her head under my chin.

"The fact that you get that is enough. Now we don't have to have that talk at least," I say, rubbing her back.

"I love you and I am sorry. I think we can make both work, maybe? Make the ceiling look like a sky, like I wanted, and add stuff to the walls to make it look like a cute little forest?" she ends in a question.

"Now that's an idea I can live with," I respond.

# GRACIE

I can't believe I acted like a child. I had this image of what I wanted in my head and didn't even consider listening to Zeke's ideas.

He's never raised his voice to me, and I could tell he was trying not to and was holding back his anger. But I felt it rolling off him. As soon as the front door slammed, the tears started to flow.

When he walked through the door with paint that I knew would be baby blue and flowers, I felt even worse. Here he was going to apologize when I was the one who was in the wrong.

It was as simple as just compromising. In the end, that's what I did and things went back to normal. He wiped the tears from my eyes and waddled with me into the kitchen so I could put the flowers in a vase.

We order pizza and eat it on the couch watching TV. Zeke ends up pulling my feet up on his lap and rubs them for me. I don't have ankles any longer. I have those dreaded cankles. I feel like I'm big as a house, but Zeke always seems to know when to compliment me or say how beautiful I am.

He also constantly has a hand on my belly and talks to the baby. I still have to pinch myself sometimes to ensure it's all real. The first time he felt the baby move, I was almost overwhelmed. The pure look of awe on his face was something I'll remember forever.

This little guy is constantly moving, too. I feel like he is using my internal organs as punching bags. I feel like I could fall asleep as Zeke continues to massage my feet. Until I get kicked or punched in the bladder. I scurry to my feet as fast as I can and waddle to the bathroom. I hear Zeke chuckling behind me. It's weird on how amused he is over how I walk.

I'm on the downslide with only three more weeks left. I have an appointment tomorrow morning to see where exactly I'm at and to just check that everything is on track.

Zeke has a bag packed already and has it sitting by the front door. He's the one that seems to be bouncing these days. We have everything for the nursey all set up, but I decided I wanted to change the paint color. I don't want to think about that again, though.

I'm washing my hands when I get sharp pain. It feel like someone is stabbing me in the back. I know that Akia had Braxton Hicks towards the end of her pregnancy, but I don't remember her saying they were much more than small cramps. This was definitely more than just a cramp. I take a deep breath and place my hands on the sink. The pain subsides so I proceed to go back to the living room.

Akia was correct in her predictions, by the way. She had a beautiful baby girl. I got to watch her one afternoon and loved every minute of it. She was completely calm and sweet the whole time. I don't know if I'm going to be that lucky based on Zeke and my personalities.

I make it to the couch and that pain hits me again making me bend over. Zeke gets up and straddles the chaise lounge pulling me down in front of him. I have my hands on my knees and I'm doing that breathing thing I learned in Lamaze. Zeke is rubbing my back and I can hear that he's called the doctor.

"Hi, this is Zeke Boyd. Gracie just had what I think may have been a contraction..." he says. I hold up two fingers not quite able to talk. "...make that two."

"She was just in the bathroom so I'm not sure, but it probably takes her a minute or two to get from there to the living room," he says, still rubbing my back.

"Okay...yeah we have a bag packed. Sure...thanks, Doc. Well, she says that we should start timing them, if they really are contractions. She's concerned that they seem to be so close already, but if they continue to occur within five minutes of each other and last longer than a minute, we should come to the hospital. She also says to come immediately if your water breaks, of course," he says with excitement in his voice.

I finally get my breath and lean back against him. He places both hands on my belly and I immediately feel a hard kick.

"I think he may be ready to get out of there. He's been kicking more than normal today. Whew, that hurts. I sure hope these are contractions, because if they aren't, I don't want to feel a real one," I say. "This is really comfortable, but I'm afraid that my water might break and I really don't want to ruin this couch. I love this couch." I sigh just as another pain shoots through me, making me bend back over.

"Okay, that was less than five minutes. Tell me when the pain stops. I've got the timer going on my phone," he says, wiggling out from behind me, standing and jogging to the kitchen.

I reach down and stop the timer at thirty seconds once the pain stops. I start laughing as Zeke comes back from the kitchen with garbage bags in his hands.

"Just in case," he says shrugging his shoulder. He helps me stand and places the bags over the seat of the couch and sets me back on. He then goes back to straddling behind me.

"Only thirty seconds. Damn that hurts," I say, snuggling back against Zeke.

This continues for the next hour. The contractions are consistent and don't seem to be getting closer, but Zeke wants to call the doctor again to check.

"She says to come on in, babe, and she'll meet us there," he yells as he runs into the kitchen. I hear him pound on Pam's door and yell, "Baby is coming! We are heading to the hospital."

I hear her yell back to go ahead that she'll call Bruce as he comes running back. As he helps me to my feet, I feel a gush between my legs.

"I think my water just broke," I say, looking down and back up to Zeke.

"Okay, we got this. Everything is going to be okay," he says as he disappears up the steps.

"Zeke, you are going the wrong way," I yell.

He comes down the steps holding a pair of sweat pants. I realize that he got me something clean to change into. *How awesome is this man?*

He helps me out of my wet leggings and helps me slip on the sweat pants. "Thank you. I don't know what I did to deserve a man like you, but you are amazing."

He gets me secured in the truck as another contraction hits me. Within seconds, he's in the truck rubbing my back and flying down the driveway.

"Let's go have us a baby."

## ZEKE

I hate seeing her in pain, but I can't help my excitement. I'm going to be meeting my son soon. I just hope she's not in labor forever.

In between timing her contractions, I was searching the internet to make sure there isn't going to be any issues with her or the baby since she's three weeks early.

From what I can see, the lungs should already be developed so I'm not worried. I wish I could do something to take away the pain, though.

Everything progresses very quickly once we get to the hospital. It was a total blur, even though it was still a few hours before my son entered the world.

At eleven twenty-one, Luke Matthew Boyd came kicking and screaming his head off into the world. Weighing six pounds three ounces, he was the tiniest, most beautiful little boy. The doctor joked that he's lungs were definitely fine and I had to agree. For being so tiny, he could certainly make a lot of noise.

I wipe the sweat off Gracie's forehead and give her a kiss. "Thank you. He's incredible. You did so well. Do you need anything?"

"Just to hold him. I want to see him. Is he okay? He certainly sounds okay," she says with a smile.

"He's perfect and definitely my boy. This kid is hung," I say, joking and puffing out my chest.

"Only you," she laughs.

"Hey, that's pretty important to a man you know. He's going to be a lady killer," I say, looking over as they finish cleaning him up and wrapping him in a blanket.

I sit on the side of the bed and wrap one arm around Gracie's shoulders pulling her against me. A nurse brings a still screaming Luke over and places him in Gracie's arms.

Instantly, he goes quiet and starts smacking his lips. I stare in amazement as Gracie pulls out a breast and see Luke latch on and start sucking. To see this instant connection is absolutely the most incredible thing I've ever witnessed. With a kiss to her head and a squeeze of her shoulder, I place a hand on my son's head as he goes to town feeding. I get a lump in my throat and try to swallow it down.

## GRACIE

Holy crap did that hurt. As soon as Zeke sits down and takes me in his arms the pain starts to subside. When little Luke is placed in my arms and stops screaming, I feel nothing but complete love. I see him smacking his lips and instinct seems to take over. Latching on, he starts eating and if there was any tinge of pain left, it's completely gone.

Zeke pulls me in closer and places a hand on Luke's head. Nothing could be better than this moment right here. Zeke was right, Luke is absolutely perfect. He has a little bit of fuzz on his head that looks to be between my color and Zeke's.

I laugh as Luke stops feeding and lets out a huge yawn and makes a face. I place him on my shoulder and pat his back and he burps and farts at the same time.

"He's definitely your son," I say laughing.

Our parents walk in with Pam, who they get situated in one of the chairs. I hand Luke over to Zeke and he immediately knows what I'm silently asking him to do.

Walking over to Pam, he places Luke in her arms with an introduction. "Great Gram Pam, meet Luke Matthew."

She raises him up and places a soft kiss on his sleeping head. "Hello there, little man. I'm going to spoil the hell out of you." Her aged and crooked fingers run over his still flushed cheeks.

I can't stop the tears. This is such an incredible moment. My adopted grandmother holding my son with such tenderness. I'm so happy to see Zeke take out his phone and take several pictures to capture this moment.

## ZEKE

They sure do push you out of the hospital quick these days. We were only in there for a total of twenty-four hours before they were wheeling Gracie and Luke out the front door.

We get home and get Luke settled in. I knew that having a newborn was not going to be easy, but damn, I didn't expect the house to be filled with a constant stream of crying. The only time he seems to not scream is when he's feeding or sleeping. Unfortunately, he's only sleeping a few hours at a time. My mom joked that he is exactly like me and that pay backs are a bitch. Everyone keeps that same mantra up about him being my mini me.

I'm on paternity leave, but I still put in a few hours in my home office. I was working a case before the birth that I can't let go. I thought the cases in Texas were rough. Being so close to D.C., I've had some really tough ones.

I don't think of myself as being that guy who is constantly horny. However, knowing we have to wait to have sex seems to cause me to have a constant painful erection. I can take care of it myself, but man it's just not the same as the feeling of being inside of Gracie

I shut down my computer and notice that the house appears to be quiet. I let out a sigh of relief and lean my head back in my office chair and close my eyes.

My hand drifts down between my legs and I palm myself through my sweat pants. Lifting the elastic, I slide my hand inside taking myself into my hand.

I feel her before I see her as my chair spins to the side. Gracie smiles as she bends over giving me a kiss with all lips and tongue. I feel myself grow harder in my hand. She uses the arms of the chair to lower herself to her knees. She runs her hands down my chest and to the waistband of my pants, pulling them down. I raise up a little to allow her to move them over my ass and down over my knees. I start stroking myself faster.

I throw my head back and let out a groan when I feel her lips wrap around the tip. It's still not the same as being deep inside her, but it's still her and it's still her mouth.

I silently pray that she does that special thing that she does to me, and I feel her hand slip down and cup my balls. I feel them tighten as she massages my ass with her finger. When she breaches the opening, I slam both hands down on the arm of the chair and try not to thrust up. I feel that familiar tingle run down my spine as she continues to go down on me and slowly move her finger in and out of my ass.

I place my hand softly on the top of her head and push her down for her to take me further into her mouth. The guttural growl that comes out of me is almost scary as I let loose and empty myself down her throat. She removes her hand from between my legs and gives me one final lick and suck. The tingle shoots through me and I can't take it anymore. I reach down and grab her under her armpits and pull her up onto my lap.

"Damn, sweet girl, that was amazing. Thank you. I didn't realize how much I needed that," I say, giving her a kiss.

"Babe, I can understand completely. I can't believe we have to wait so long to have sex. Right now, it feels like my nether regions are on fire though," she says, pulling my head to her chest.

"We can't have sex, but you just proved that we can do other things," I say wiggling my eyebrows. "I can suck on your clit for a while."

"You'll have to give me a while to heal. I can't even imagine you anywhere near there right now. I'll be fine," she says laughing.

Just at that moment we hear the familiar cries of Luke through the whole house.

"I got him. He's hungry, I'm sure," Gracie says standing.

"I'll go with you. I'll change him first. I'm sure he's got a dirty diaper as well," I respond.

We get ourselves situated and climb the steps hand in hand. I lift Luke out of his crib and proceed to change his diaper as Gracie situates herself in the rocking chair. After I hand him over and he dives in, I sit on the floor and watch her feed my son. I don't think I'll ever stop thinking that this is the most beautiful thing a mother can do for her child.

Every two hours we run upstairs and go through the same routine. I change him and hand him over for Gracie to feed him. I take a seat on the floor with my back against the dresser and just watch them. It truly is a beautiful sight.

We finally get him settled and asleep and both drag ourselves to bed. It feels like I just laid my head down when the cries echo off the walls. I know he's not hungry but he may need to be changed. I tell Gracie to stay and sleep. She mumbles out a thank you and rolls over.

I go into Luke's room and lift him out of the crib. He definitely has a full diaper, so I clean him up and get him into a new one. I was told that a father needs to bond with their kid and skin to skin in normally the best way. He's lying on the changing table in just his new diaper, so I slip my shirt over my head. His still fussing and wide awake as I pick him up and press him against my chest. It's almost three in the morning, and I'm exhausted. I would give anything for him to fall back to sleep.

I sit down in the rocking chair. We are bare chest to bare chest. I place a gentle kiss to the top of his head and start singing softly. His cries soften as I rock and sing. I feel as he takes a deep breath and lets out a little whimper on the exhale, but he goes completely limp in my arms. I continue to softly sing to him when I see Gracie appear in the doorway. She leans her head against the door jamb and smiles. I'm afraid to stop rocking and singing. So, I continue but now I'm singing to Gracie. I sing a song called "Sleeping Beauty" and I see a tear fall from her eye. There's a part where it says that I hope your dreams come true and she nods her head.

I place Luke in his crib and he remains motionless and content. I walk over and pull Gracie into my arms.

"That was beautiful and yes, my dreams have come true, because of you. You are an amazing husband and father. I can't imagine my life without you," she says.

Amazingly, Luke sleeps until almost nine the next morning. He almost seems like something changed. He's less fussy and seems more cooperative with us. I continue to remove my shirt and his when I hold him, thinking that maybe that had something to do with it. I have no clue but over time, he begins to cry less and sleep more. I know that babies eventually get a schedule, but inside I think that I have something to do with it. Hey, it's a guy thing. Just let us have this moment, even if it's not real.

# EPILOGUE
## *Solace*

## ZEKE

I can't believe how my life has come full circle. The suffocation that I felt growing up now seems unreal. The past few years have been nothing less than amazing. Seeing my family when I want and experiencing all the little moments of each other lives has meant so much to me.

We ended up taking our honeymoon a year later. It doesn't seem that we ever do anything in the right order. As expected, we both really enjoyed the resort. Having our families there was a bit awkward in some instances, but overall it was a great experience. I loved seeing Rachel and the old crew again. Dad and I sang a few songs together. I thought that I was going to miss it, but I really don't. I enjoy singing sometimes at family events, but I'm just as happy strumming the guitar for just Gracie and me.

We welcomed a little girl into the fold nine months later. Rebecca Grace was totally opposite to Luke. She never fussed or cried and slept through the night almost immediately. Luke just loved his baby sister. He was just two, but I saw a change in him like he knew he was responsible for her. Nothing could make a father prouder than to see his son display such values while being so young. When she did cry, we would find Luke in her bedroom, and sometimes even in her crib, holding her hand and humming to her.

Standing with my arms on the top of the fence of the corral, I watch as Gracie leads a horse around with Becca perched on top. Luke is on his own horse, making laps around them. He's been riding on his own since he was five. He's told me and Gracie that he's going to be a champion barrel racer. I have little doubt that he won't accomplish this one day. The way he handles a horse at seven is pretty amazing.

Becca isn't as secure as Luke and is, and still insistent on Gracie taking the reins and leading. I'm okay with this as I tend to be a little more protective of my little girl. I mean, she's only five and still a baby as far as I'm concerned.

Luke is my splitting image but with hair. I see the same fire in his eyes that my dad says I had growing up. Dad always said I wouldn't understand how he felt until I had a boy. He was right. I know Luke is probably going to want to get out of this town and experience things just like I wanted to. I just hope he doesn't stay away as long as I did.

I look back on the moment where I felt full of dread to have to come home and am so thankful that I did. I met this beautiful woman who became my wife and mother of my children. Her eyes meet mine and she smiles. It's a smile that I feel.

Some people question what their purpose is in life. I know mine. It's right in front of me and it's simple. To be the best husband and father that I can be.

**THE END**

# ACKNOWLEDGEMENTS

There are so many people that I want to thank. I have three fantastic women who was there for me through this entire book. Stephanie, Pam, and Brook. They've been a part of the whole series and their encouragement and enthusiasm always kept me going.

Of course, you the reader. Thank you for choosing to read my story. I would love to see your reviews and feedback.

A big thank you to Reggie Deanching who was wonderful to work with and has an incredible eye. I was heading in a totally different direction, but seeing that post with that picture, Zeke was born. Reggie actually had a hand in the title, too. The photo caption was solace in solitude. How amazing is that?

Of course, thanks to Matthew Hosea who not only is in the cover photo, but provided me tons of visual inspirations. The only thing I think I left out was the tattoo of the donkey on his ass. But seriously, Matthew has an amazing voice, too.

And lastly to Lee Brice. No, I don't know him, but his song "Boy" was the other inspiration. The first time I heard the song after I decided to buy the photo, (which was on the same day) the entire story practically unfolded in my head. So, I have to acknowledge him.

# FINDING SOLACE PLAYLIST

Boy......Lee Brice
Learn my lesson......Daughtry
Little Things......One Direction
What Makes You Beautiful......One Direction
You and Me.....Lifehouse
Wanted....Hunter Hayes
Sunday Morning.....Parmalee
Sleeping Beauty......Dylan Scott
She's Got This Thing About Her........Chris Young
Woman, Amen ..................Dierks Bentley

Made in the USA
Middletown, DE
28 September 2022